I0608010

CAPTIVE MAGIC

MYSTIC'S END MYSTERIES BOOK 8

LEANNE LEEDS

BADCHEN PUBLISHING

Captive Magic
Published by Badchen Publishing
14125 W State Highway 29
Suite B-203 119
Liberty Hill, TX 78642 USA

CAPTIVE MAGIC

ONE

It felt like there were hundreds of them. Maybe even thousands. Their deaths crossed over a span of two hundred years. Two hundred years of damage from one woman's curse on this little town. Damage continued by her descendants —culminating in my mother.

A curse I—and my two newly-discovered sisters —had been working diligently to reverse, bottle by bottle. Even though we, technically, were descendants of the first traitor witch, too.

In reality, we'd found only twenty-six ghosts since we began—the last twenty or so discovered over the past few months in rapid succession. Twenty-six women of Mystic's End, Arkansas. It was an achievement, to be sure, since the strange curse with murky origins had been plaguing the town for years. I wasn't sure why my arrival in the town had sped up its unraveling so quickly. It didn't seem like my being a descendant of the curser and inheritor of the power of the cursee should have broken the whole thing wide open.

But, well, it did.

"I'm telling you, there's gotta be only one bottle left," Miss Bessie (d. 2020) told the group while exchanging a look with her daughter, Mary. Mary (d. 1990) wore a pinched expression while glancing out over the crowded room. "There's barely a shield left on this town. You can wave your hand right through it," the old woman reminded them. "One more, and we'll all be able to fly to Hawaii for the holidays. Mark my words."

"I'll mark your words, Bessie, but that doesn't mean there's only one bottle left," Catherine Richter (d. 1972) responded. "There could be two or three. Perhaps it's just a small number with little energy to power the anchored spells."

"And perhaps the old woman doesn't know what she's talking about," Plum Korzybski (d. 1981), a striking young woman with a shock of midnight blue hair, retorted hastily. "Wasn't she the one that thought Gabe had to marry Fortuna? If you ask me, she's out of her depth. Her opinions carry no more weight than anyone else's. I don't know why everyone treats her like the expert here. We were the ones in the damn bottles."

Miss Bessie looked offended.

"Ladies, perhaps we can dial back the animosity?" I called over the din of disagreement. "Bickering over how close we are to breaking the curse completely will not get us any closer to our goal. One bottle at a time. That's how we've gotten this far; that's how you're all here. That's what we need to focus on. Agreed?"

"No. We need to focus on getting Anna out of that stupid white rock she's in," Plum disagreed.

"I agree with Plum," Spike added quickly.

Of course, Spike agreed with Plum. Plum could suggest the moon was made of cheese, and Spike would nod his head in total agreement. Ever since the punk rock girl had popped out of her bottle, my original mohawked ghost roommate followed her around the way sunlight tracks the shadow of a cloud.

"There is one thing they're right about," Dalida said as she leaned forward.

"Which they? Miss Bessie, or the other ghosts?"

"It might be time to see if we can chisel Anna out of the selenite," Angie, my younger sister, finished for Dalida. "If the shield keeping the ghosts here has become thin, we might be able to bust her out of that thing."

"I hear you, but I'm still not sure about that." I shifted in my chair, turning away from the room filled with ghosts. "She's alive in that thing, Angie. What if we hurt her?" I shook my head, no. "As horrible as it is that she's still in it, I don't want to take the chance. Do you really want to explain to Martin that you stabbed his mother accidentally? How do you think that will affect your relationship?"

Angie frowned. "Well—no, I guess not."

Dalida sighed. "Maybe Fortuna is right. It feels slow, I agree, but we've made such incredible progress over the past couple of months. I mean, look at all these people."

The three of us turned and looked at the bickering, arguing, frowning ghosts.

* * *

Later that night, Chris and I sat around a crackling campfire. I wasn't exactly sure where we were. This place, a cave somewhere deep in the Ouachita Mountains of Arkansas, was a refuge precisely because it was hard to find. It was far from Mystic's End, and the walls sparkled with crystals embedded in the mountains, blocking it from prying magical eyes. Chris and I used it frequently to get away from it all.

He passed me a plate holding my weekly Beef Wellington, a side of buttery mashed potatoes, and perfectly broiled asparagus. Though we'd long passed the point of bribery in exchange for a date, the vampire had promised me fancy weekly restaurant food if I agreed to go out with him. I would not turn down my favorite dish.

"It's still hard to get used to," I told him between unladylike bites. "You not eating, I mean."

"There's only one thing in this cave that I can eat now," my vampire boyfriend told me with a gleam in his eye.

My fork stopped mid-lift. "Okay, that was kinda gross."

He laughed. "I actually regretted it as soon as I said that. Double entendres being what they are, and all."

I put down my fork. "Okay, you've made it twice as gross as I originally thought it was."

"Sorry, I'll stop trying to be amusing." Chris's expression grew serious. "You look tired. Are you getting enough sleep?"

The answer was no, but I didn't want him to worry about me.

My three-story brownstone was filled with twenty-seven ghosts that always had opinions they wanted to share. My business, an art studio on the first floor, was effectively being run by my art student Azalea Cotton—because I barely had any time to spend on it anymore. Every other day I ran back and forth between the greyhound track and Mystic Moon Gallery to help Martin adopt out the last greyhounds. Between all that, I spent time with my best friend, reporter Pepper Stanford, at the library trying to figure out where the last bottle—or last few bottles—might be hidden.

Oh. And the only time I could see my boyfriend was after the sun went down and before the sun went up.

So, yeah. I didn't even know what sleep was anymore.

"Don't worry about me," I told him, smiling. "I'll be fine."

Chris tilted his head. "That wasn't an answer. I was worried about this."

"You were worried about what?" I asked him while continuing to demolish the steak wrapped in mushrooms and pate and flaky pastry. "I'm sure I'm getting enough sleep. If I wasn't, I would've vomited on you on the way here." My vampire boyfriend could grab me and sail me across miles in just minutes—an experience that almost always left me with nausea and vertigo. "Almost sure of it." I swallowed and smiled. He looked at me, still concerned, and I blurted out, "Fine. The ghosts are driving me nuts, I don't even know what's going on in my business, I can't find the last stupid bottle, and I miss you during the day. Happy?"

"I don't know if happy would be the right word." Chris's intense, dark eyes flickered for just a moment with pain. "I am glad you told me the truth. Finally. Getting much faster at that lately, too."

"Watch it," I warned him. I couldn't resist teasing him. He knew me too well now, and it wasn't always the most comfortable position to be in.

He winked. "You know, we could solve this issue completely by simply turning you."

"Turning me into what?" I asked flippantly.

"You know what. We've discussed it before. You would have boundless energy, a defined sleeping schedule. You'd keep your witch magic— your mother had vampire-witch hybrids that were incredibly powerful. It's not all that bad, really. In fact, I'm quite happy they turned me into a vampire. It's quite useful."

"Except for the whole drinking human blood thing, right?" I pointed to my Beef Wellington. "I'd have to give this up. Not only that, I wanted to go to Hawaii all my life. It's a vacation I haven't taken yet. All my life, Sparkles. I'm going to take that vacation, and it won't be the same if I can't go to the beach and sunbathe."

"Beaches are beautiful at night, you know." Chris smiled widely.

I put down my plate and looked across the fire at him. "Look, I know you're playing this off like a joke, and I'm not offended by the suggestion. You're charming about it, and I know you would never push me into doing something I hadn't decided to do. I'm not against vampires. You are who you are, and I love who you are—" I tensed up once I realized I basically told this debonair vampire I loved him—something I wasn't ready to say.

Not a muscle moved on his face. If he caught it, he didn't acknowledge it.

I paused, swallowed, and took a deep breath. "Look, me turning into a vampire is the paranormal equivalent of a marriage proposal between us." I looked into his eyes. "And you know it."

"It doesn't have to be," Chris responded. "It's something I think would make your life easier."

"For the first time in my life, I like who I am. Heck, for the first time in my life, I know who I am."

"I would never want to change that."

"I know you wouldn't. And I know that your suggestion is coming from a place of care for me, and I appreciate it. I really do. But that's not the only place it's coming from, Sparkles." He opened his mouth to argue, but I raised my hand to stop him. "And even if I'm wrong about that? My convenience and getting more sleep are not why I would make that kind of decision. And you know it. You're the only vampire I know, and you're making the offer." I tilted my head. "I wouldn't enter into a tie like that lightly. You understand? We've only been dating a couple of months."

"Like I said, I would never want to push you into doing something you weren't ready for. Luckily, I'm a vampire, and I have all the time in the world. Immortality has its benefits." He gave me a reassuring smile. "As to the discussion at hand, if there's anything I can do to help you with your burdens, you know you have but to ask."

"I appreciate that." I held up my glass. "Any wine?"

* * *

"How did it go?" My younger sister, Angie, sat on the bed, reading a magazine.

Besides my three-story home being haunted by twenty-six women and one punk rock guy, my two sisters had moved in. Dalida, my fraternal twin, had been staying with me since our mother had blown up her living room—long story. Angie joined us within two weeks thanks to a profound case of FOMO—fear of missing out.

"It's always good to spend time with him," I told

her. Gideon, my greyhound, followed me around the bedroom as I put down my purse and stripped off the layers of warm clothes I always wore when Chris and I visited the cave. "He brought up my turning into a vampire again."

"Yeah, but did he do it on one knee with a ruby ring?" Angie chuckled. "If he didn't? I say no way."

Across the room on her bed, Dalida clucked her tongue. "You just can't get rid of the gold digger thing, can you?"

"I don't need to dig gold, sister dear. I have Scrooge McDuck levels of my own, and when Martin asks me to marry him, will have a combined net worth of...of..." Angie looked up at the ceiling and counted on her fingers. After a few moments, she shrugged and gave up. "Well, it will be a lot. I just think if Sparkles wants our sister to join him in some immortal bloodbath, he should make it a little romantic and propose formally. Like a normal person."

"But he's not a normal person," Dalida told her. "He's a vampire."

"I've heard nothing about vampires bursting into flames as soon as they cross the threshold of a jewelry store. I'm just saying." Angie turned and snapped her fingers at Gideon. "Dog, get your nose out of Fortuna's purse!"

Gideon, his face buried up to his ears in my

leather handbag, yanked his head out with a bag clutched firmly between his teeth.

"Oh, shoot, I forgot about the bacon Chris gave me for him." After a tug-of-war that was harder than it needed to be, Gideon was happily scarfing down bacon slices while I picked up pieces of the ripped white paper bag from my bedroom floor. "Look, it's not about a ring or a formal proposal or anything like that. Chris and I have been dating for just two months."

"Martin and I have been dating for three," Angie interjected.

"And Gabe and I have been dating for two," Dalida added. "And you're a telepath to boot. What's your point?"

"Would either of you turn into vampires for them?" I put on my pajamas and sat down on my bed. "First, I don't know if I want to be a vampire. Sure, lots of stuff about it is kind of cool. But then you add in that killed by the sun and drinking blood thing, and suddenly? Not so cool."

Dalida shook her head. "If you don't do something, you're going to collapse from exhaustion. You're burning the binding candle at both ends, here, Fortuna. I know I've said it before, and I'll repeat it—you don't have to do everything by yourself."

"I'm not doing everything by myself!" Sure, in

the past, I had problems with letting other people help. Or allowing them to participate. Or telling them what I was thinking. Or, um, listening to other people.

But that was in the past!

"You and Pepper are buried in that library with Irma all afternoon. You go off with Chris every other night searching for bottles—"

"That's just because he's faster!" I said defensively.

"You're working with Martin on the greyhound adoption when any of us could do that. I mean, really, Fortuna—that doesn't even involve any magic. That's just organization."

"And Martin has hundreds of employees, any of them could do it," Angie added. "He told me you insisted you work on it."

"I pushed for it; I want to see it through." My answers were getting less and less emphatic because I realized they were less and less defensible. My sisters, both, also knew me a little too well.

I was a bit of a control freak.

"Let me take over the greyhound adoptions," Angie said as she scratched her greyhound's ears. "I know just as much about them as you do. I have one, too, and it will let me spend more time with Martin. You'd be doing me a favor."

I looked down to find the eyes of Angie's greyhound looking up at me. While my younger sister thought she knew just as much about greyhounds as I did, I knew one more thing than she did. I knew that her adopted greyhound was Ella Grayson, Angie's former friend (and sociopathic murderer).

And I knew that because I'd accidentally turned Ella Grayson into Angie's greyhound.

Well, the dog wasn't Angie's greyhound at the time. It was just dumb luck that my own sister adopted her.

I kept meaning to tell her.

I just never had time.

I sighed.

"Okay, fine, you're right, I'm spread a little thin," I admitted, plopping down on my bed. "If you can take over the rest of the greyhound adoptions, that would be great. I think there are only ten dogs left."

"Done!" Angie chirped.

"What can I do?" Dalida asked.

I sighed. "Corral the ghosts. Keep every day from turning into the world's worst, and longest, and most annoying board meeting ever. I feel like we are on the verge of having committees." I ran my hands through my hair and stared at my twin sister. "I don't want committees."

"I can do that," she nodded. "Do one thing for us, though."

I tensed. "What?"

"Shut the lights off and get some sleep."

I crawled to the head of my bed and jumped on the mattress, pulling a tangle of sheets and soft cotton blankets out from under me. "Done," I told them, yawning. I wrapped the bedding up over my shoulder as Gideon wiggled his warm body underneath my arm. With a deep breath, I was asleep in seconds.

TWO

"But where did they go?" Keziah (d. 1873) asked me the following morning before I'd finished my coffee. Actually, I'd barely taken a sip of my coffee. You would think after staying here for a few months, the witch ghosts would pick up on my needing to be halfway through a mug first thing in the morning to be useful. But apparently, they hadn't.

"The town ghosts? As in the ghosts of not-witches, you mean?"

She nodded.

"I don't know. In the beginning, it seemed sort of odd to me. I just figured it had something to do with the curse on the town and thought little more about it."

She frowned. "So, you think it's because of the curse, but you have no explanation—no theory at all —for why no ghosts are haunting Mystic's End? That doesn't seem like you at all, Fortuna."

I opened my mouth to say something and then closed it again.

In some ways, Keziah was right. The team was continually looking to me for answers (even though they usually knew just as much as I did) because I— or Pepper—tended to put all the pieces together. Here, though? It just didn't seem all that important to waste time thinking about.

Watching the steam rise from my nearly untouched morning cup of joe and yawning away the last bit of tiredness, I shrugged. "I don't know every little thing that happens in this town or the answer to every anomaly. Like I said, it didn't seem a top priority. And don't forget, there are ghosts in Mystic's End. Spike was living in this very building for years. Tom Wilson's ghost is living with his ex-wife and ex-mistress," I told her.

Keziah leaned on the counter and raked her thick, dark hair back from her face. She was incorporeal, so she wasn't really touching her hair (just the memory of hair) or leaning on the counter (she could pass right through it). I noticed, though, that the memory of life was so powerful ghosts would mimic sitting, leaning, lying down...I guess it was the same way that Chris appeared to breathe. "It just seems to me that there's something more to the absence of afterlife here." She looked around the room at the other ghosts. "We shouldn't be all there are, Fortuna. There has to be more. Souls don't simply disappear."

"Well, of course not, but don't they go somewhere?" Dalida asked, joining us. My sister placed a hand on my shoulder as if to apologize for allowing Keziah's questions to waylay me. "Heaven, the Elysian fields? Have to go somewhere, right? Maybe that's what happened. The entire town just moved on except for the few that are left."

I shrugged again. "That answer's way above my pay grade." There was a slight pause in the conversation, so I gulped my coffee down. If this was the breakfast chat this day was starting with, it would likely be another long one.

"I can't believe you two are unconcerned. We have gone, two by two, all over the length and width of this town," Keziah continued, squinting at Dalida. "As we've looked for the bottles, we've looked for others like us: other secrets, other souls, other paranormals. I say to you both—that we have found none, not a one? It is abnormal. Something is amiss."

"It doesn't seem like anything in this town is completely normal, Keziah," Dalida told the concerned ghost, a kind look on her face. "Just the fact that you are here, that Angie, Fortuna, and I have the history that we do...That Angie's father suddenly has no memory of all he learned about magic and their mother..." She paused and looked off into the distance for a moment, as though the reason everything was as it was hung in the air on the other side of the room. "This is a strange town with strange stories."

"But we know most of them now."

Dalida turned and raised her eyebrow. "You think so, sister?" She glanced down at Angie's greyhound and chuckled. "You haven't even told Angie that her dog is a transmogrified murderer."

The hint of a frown crossed my forehead. "I'm going to tell her. Eventually."

"It's been two months. You're not going to tell her." Dalida dismissed my assertion.

"I just don't know how to explain that her beloved pet is her crazy ex-friend Ella Grayson. I mean, if I had told her a few months ago, it probably would've been easier. But then I put it off. And I put it off some more."

"And I agreed to hide it from her," Dalida added faintly. "Something I still can't believe I did."

"We were brand-new sisters!" I chirped. "You didn't want to make me mad."

"As I've gotten to know you and Angie, Fortuna,

I should have been fine letting you be angry at me. Our younger sister has a bit of a fiery temper, in case you haven't noticed. She's the one I should be wary of."

"Of course, I've noticed. She pushed Spike down the stairs and killed him," I pointed out genially.

"I did not!" Angie retorted as she pushed her way into our discussion. "It was an accident. I don't know how many times I have to tell you it was an accident, but you know? I think you bring that whole thing up more than Spike does! Get over it, Fortuna."

"Your sister knows about accidents," Keziah said with a clever eyebrow raise.

"Are you kidding? Miss Perfect over here?" Angie glanced over at me and stuck her tongue out. "When have you ever made a mistake? Had an accident? Colored outside the lines?"

Keziah, Dalida, and I immediately looked at Angie's dog.

Angie's eyes narrowed. "Why is everybody looking at my dog?"

* * *

Beulah Conroe swept into my store right after my second cup of coffee.

I was—mercifully—upstairs in a meeting with Dalida, Angie, Bessie, and Mary, plotting out our next search grid to look for the last bottle. Poor Azalea looked haggard as she came up to the second floor and apologized profusely for bothering me. "She just won't tell me what she wants, Fortuna," Azalea explained, her eyes wide. "I've asked a hundred different times, it feels like, and the woman just refuses to talk to me."

"Did she ask for me specifically?"

"No, not...not by name," the young artist responded, shifting uncomfortably.

I blinked. "Okay, I'll bite. What does that mean?"

"She used some language that I would rather not repeat." Azalea's cheeks pinked up. "If that's okay."

Dalida, Angie, and I looked at one another. "Okay, I'll be right down."

Azalea nodded and hurried down the steps.

"Who's Beulah Conroe?" Dalida asked.

"She's a member of the Grace Gang at Holy Grove Church," Angie told Dalida with a frown. "The Grace Gang is this group of three old women who have nothing better to do than get into everyone's business. They are the most judgmental, horrible, pseudo-pious—"

I raised my eyebrow. "I take it you've had a run-in with them?"

"You mean because I'm the former town lush? Or because I ran off to Hollywood?" Angie sat back and posed in a sultry manner. "Or because my first husband was super old, and I was super young, and he died, and I became super-rich? Or because—"

"I think we got it," Dalida said, cutting her off.

Angie shot Dalida a humorless smile. "But yes. The Grace Gang has tried to save my soul. It was decidedly unpleasant." She wrinkled her pixie nose.

Before Angie discovered she was our sister—the product of an affair between our mother and the father who raised her—she'd had many problems she tried to drink away. On top of the inherent difficulties that come with being perpetually drunk, Angie'd been angry when she drank. Her verbal assaults on people—including me—were legendary, and her reputation in the town was not the best.

I detested her. Once.

Miss Bessie had told me I didn't know her full story, and the old woman had been right. Angie had no idea she had inherited paranormal powers. My younger sister, the sultry spitfire lush, was actually a powerful empathic healer. Her touch could take away pain or sadness or darkness in an instant. It had been, we realized, the reason her first husband loved her so much. She had taken away the intense anguish caused by his illness and replaced it with bliss. That kind of thing could make anyone fall in love.

Once Angie discovered the truth about herself, it seemed to settle her.

Well, mostly.

"I guess I should go talk to her," I said with a reluctance that all could see.

"You need to close this business," Angie told me with a toss of her head. "We all have more than enough money to live the life of rich socialites. Why are you even keeping this place open? I mean, why bother?"

My younger sister wasn't wrong. Well, about her and Dalida, at least. Angie had millions thanks to her first husband (who had been childless). Dalida had a somewhat cordial relationship with her own adoptive parents, and they provided a substantial trust fund for her comfort. But I left my rich, adopted parents when I was barely sixteen without taking a dime from them. While my two sisters might not need to work, I did.

"If you don't have to work, why bother keeping the club open?" Angie owned and held court at The Centre Club, an overly fancy rotating restaurant at Martin's entertainment complex.

"It's not like anyone else's gonna let me on stage to sing," my sister shot back.

"Well, I enjoy painting, and I enjoy having the shop," I told her with a shrug. "And I am not independently wealthy the way the two of you are, so I have to keep my business running. If Beulah Conroe wants to learn how to paint beautiful paintings, I'm happy to sell her the supplies or tell her when to show up for class." I pushed off the counter and headed toward the stairwell. "This shouldn't take too long. Just let me help her with what she needs."

"Maybe you should find out what name she called you before you decide to take her on as your next art student," Dalida called after me.

* * *

"And Reverend Kane thought you were a lost sheep," Beulah Conroe said as I emerged into the storefront. "I once told you when you came to the church, we shoot wolves in these here parts. Didn't take the hint, did ya?"

Her tone stopped me in my tracks. I stared at the woman, surprised by the animosity coming off her.

When I didn't reply, she gave Azalea a stern look. "I think it's time for you to go into the back."

Azalea froze, staring back at the silver-haired old woman. "Now!" she added when Azalea didn't move, her voice dripping with menace.

"Azalea, why don't you go get the studio set up for this afternoon's class," I told the girl in a friendly, casual voice. Usually, I would jump all over anyone that talked to my staff that way, elderly woman or not. After Beulah's opening, though, I sensed it was safer for the girl to be as far away from this conversation as I could get her. "I'll let you know when I need you up front again."

"Okay," she responded quickly and bolted into the back.

When Azalea was safely two rooms away, I whirled back toward the old woman. "Just what on earth do you think you're doing coming in here and talking to her like that?" I asked the cantankerous old woman. "That young woman did nothing to you, and that was no way to treat her."

"I don't know who you think you are, talking to me that way, but I will not be spoken to in this manner by a Delphi hussy," Beulah spat back, her nose so far in the air that if she walked out in the rain, she would drown.

"You won't be spoken to in this manner?" I asked, laughing. "Ma'am, have you listened to yourself lately?"

"We waited two months for our donation,"

Beulah spat, holding up two fingers and thrusting them at me. "Two months, we struggled, and it's your fault! You're the reason our church might go under!"

"I...Your church?" I blinked. "What do I have to do with your church?"

"Your mother has been donating to our fine house every month for years," Beulah explained, the haughty arrogance never missing from her tone. "She told Reverend Kane that she won't hand over another penny until her daughter comes and talks to her." The old woman's watery eyes narrowed. "That's you. How you could come from so fine, so pious a woman, I will never know. But you've got to fix this, young lady. You've got to fix this right now."

I suspected my face looked shocked, and my mouth was probably gaping open like a fish. My mother donated monthly to the Holy Grove Church? Why would she do that? How long had it been going on? And why had Ollie, Rev. Kane's son, said nothing about this? My mind raced in a hundred directions at once.

When I didn't respond, Beulah Conroe shot me an angry look. "Well?"

"Are you telling me that the Holy Grove Church is entirely funded by Karen White?"

"Didn't I just say that?" the old woman asked.

"And Reverend Kane has gone to see Karen White in jail?"

"I just said that, too!" Beulah responded angrily. "You have cotton in your ears?"

"And Karen White said until I go visit her in jail, she won't donate to your church anymore?"

Beulah Conroe clenched her teeth. "Are you just going to repeat everything I said back to me?"

"Until I understand it, honestly, I just might," I said, scratching my head. "If this has been going on for two months, why are you just now coming to me? And if she told that to Reverend Kane, why is he not here? And what about my other two sisters? She doesn't want to see them?"

"She wants to talk to the one that's dating the blood devil," Beulah hissed, and then made many signs on herself after she said the words blood devil. "That's you. And I'm sure you don't care, but Reverend Kane doesn't understand what's going on. He's afraid that because your sister is dating Martin, approaching you would make Martin angry. You've made a vigorous man afraid, you Delphi hussy!"

"Why is my mother donating to your church?" I asked her, my tone not bothering to hide my suspicion. "What is it you and your church are doing for her?"

"That's none of your business," she snapped back.

For a time, we stared at one another in mutual consternation. The gray-haired woman resented having to come here, and I could feel it snapping off her like fireworks. And she really disliked me.

I pushed within her mind to examine what she held there, what secrets she was hiding from me.

There was fear. A deep sorrow that this church she cared about so much was so very threatened. A fury that to save it, she had to come and speak to the likes of me.

But there was another, darker agenda just below that.

A nugget of truth, a fact, floating just beneath the murky depths of her fury.

It was cloaked, and I couldn't pull it out no matter how hard I tried. Maybe Beulah Conroe didn't even know what was hiding out within her own mind. That's how secret, buried and protected it was.

Which meant it was hidden, buried, and protected by magic.

Great.

THREE

Just when I thought the day could get no more complicated, Pepper raced into my shop waving her cell phone. "I just got a call from Ollie. You're not going to believe what happened."

"Well, Ms. Stanford, funny you should show up. I've got a story for you, too," I replied with a wave of my hand. "Beulah Conroe was just here. She claims that my mother is the primary financial support behind Holy Grove Church. Since dear old mom's in jail, there have been no donations for the past two months, and they're a bit miffed. Beulah Conroe says Mom told Dexter Kane she won't cut a check unless I go see her."

"Your mother?" Pepper said, her voice louder.

"Why would your mother support that crazy church? Did she even go? And why would she pass messages to you through Rev. Kane of all people?"

"That's probably a better question for your boyfriend." Pepper Stanford and Dexter Kane's son Ollie had been dating for several months now. Much to the Right Reverend's chagrin, Ollie was a long-haired biker devoted to the local paper's star investigative reporter. "Speaking of, what's your story?"

Pepper looked confused for a moment, and then her eyes widened as if she just remembered. "Oh, right, the call from Ollie. He and Bobby Newsom went to pick up a dead body. Councilman Conrad Noble got shot. The dude was sitting right in his office, and someone popped him right between the eyes."

"Oh, no! That's horrible," I told her. I didn't know the councilman well, but I had met him once or twice at the track. He was a balding man, small and nervous. Kind of reminded me of a weasel. "Why would someone kill him?"

Pepper shrugged and leaned against the counter, her chin in her hands. "His secretary found the body this morning. As far as I know, no one's been arrested. But that's not the crazy part. That's not even the million-dollar question. Go on." She batted her eyes at me. "Ask me the million-dollar question. Oh, you'll never guess. But try. No, no, you'll never guess. It'll knock your socks off."

I tried to jump into the conversation Pepper seemed to be having with herself. "Okay, what's the million-dollar question?"

"The million-dollar question is why the nerdy pencil pusher was found dead in his office clutching the very last witch bottle in his cold, stiff hand." Pepper stood up and held her hands out. "Ollie found the last witch bottle. Granted, that's the good news." She frowned. "The bad news is that last part —that he found it in a murder victim's hands. Now it's in evidence."

I blinked in shock. "Is Ollie sure it's a witch bottle?"

Pepper rolled her eyes and tapped on her phone. Turning the screen toward me, she held up a picture of the dead councilman. His fingers were wrapped around a purple bottle that clearly resembled the twenty-six other witch bottles we had found around Mystic's End. "You tell me," Pepper said. "You're the expert. He says he's ninety-nine point nine percent sure it's the last bottle. We've been looking all over for these. He can tell."

"It looks like it could be," I said as I examined it, my voice low. "It's hard to tell from the picture, though." I looked up. "Can we get close to it?"

"Right, again, that was the whole bad news part? Remember? The dead guy was clutching it. When he died." Pepper stared at me, and I gazed back at her, waiting. "They put it into evidence."

"When has that ever stopped you before?" Pepper Stanford had illegal access to the police cage in the back of the Mystic's End library—and probably a lot more places I didn't know about (and didn't want to know about). I found it hard to believe that she couldn't get me to the bottle.

"This is different," Pepper explained, frowning. "This is actual physical evidence. It's going to go into the dungeon of the new Mystic's End Police Department. Thanks to Martin's generous donation toward construction costs, the place is a fortress."

"Doesn't Ollie have access?" I asked. "He's the assistant coroner. Doesn't his boss do the inquest?"

Pepper shook her head. "They shot the guy in the face. There's really not a question; this is a murder. I suspect Bobby Newsom did the paperwork in the truck on the way back to the morgue. He doesn't have to spend much effort on this one."

"Okay, then how do we get near the bottle?" I asked, crossing my arms.

"Your sister is the daughter of the chief of police," Pepper pointed out. "I'd suggest asking her for some ideas. They'll probably be a bit more legal than mine."

* * *

"He remembers nothing about what he's gone through the past few months," Gabe said as the six of us sat around the table later that afternoon. We were discussing the ways we could get our hands on the last witch bottle. "It's not like you can just walk in and ask your father for access to the evidence room. He will not give it to you. You have no explanation for why you would want it, anyway."

"My dad would do anything for me," Angie said confidently.

"I disagree," Gabe told her, his face serious. "Your father's confused enough as it is with the political upheaval in this town of late, and the Mayor's been all over him about the greyhound track closing, losing revenue. Not to mention his arrest of Karen, who donated thousands to the Mayor's campaign. He is in serious cover-his-a—"

"Okay, okay, I get it." Angie made a face. "So what do you suggest? Break into the evidence room?"

"I like her," Pepper said cheerfully, pointing at Angie with a wink. My sister winked back.

Gabe shifted in his seat. "There's no way you'd get in. It's three levels down through two security systems. This isn't a lock you can pick with a hairpin"—he glanced at Pepper—"in a few seconds."

"Very few seconds," Pepper agreed confidently.

"Look, as much as I hate to admit it, Gabe's right," Ollie agreed, looking glum. "I don't know why a small town needs an evidence locker that's as protected as that one is. Maybe they expected to have higher value evidence because of the track. For whatever reason, they restrict the evidence locker access. Even if I wanted to go down there, I couldn't. I have to make an evidence request."

"So just make an evidence request," I said.

"And if it is a witch bottle—"

"Then I uncork it, and you send it back," I told him, shrugging. "I don't understand why this is so complicated. No harm, no foul, right?"

"Except that I don't have any reason to request it anymore," Ollie disagreed. "Bobby's already ruled that it's a murder. The whole thing's been handed over to the police to investigate. Unless they ask me to test something, I don't have any reason to ask for it. I'm still just the assistant. I can commandeer testing kits, and I get away with a lot, but murder evidence?" He shook his head. "Bobby and I work in the same room. He'd know."

"I feel like everybody's getting cautious in their old age." I glared at Ollie. "A few months ago, you were hacking into security systems and stealing evidence. What the heck happened to you?"

Pepper and Ollie glanced at each other as if they had a secret.

"What's that look?" I asked sharply.

"What look?" Ollie asked. Pepper elbowed him.

"She may lie like a champ, but you can't. You're too innocent-looking," I told Ollie. "Come on, you two. Share with the class. What is this all about?"

"This is why you should always let me talk," Pepper grumbled at Ollie. She sat up straight and sighed. "I guess you guys were going to find out eventually, anyway. Ollie's decided to run for County Coroner in the fall," Pepper said as Ollie bowed his head with a sheepish grin. "He has to keep his nose clean, or he could jeopardize his chances. One thing that could jeopardize his run is getting arrested for tampering with evidence. So, he's a little more careful."

"Congratulations, dude, that's great!" Gabe said, clapping his best friend on the back. "I think you'll do an outstanding job. At the very least, you can't do a worse job than the current coroner." He smiled at Dalida and winked.

"What's wrong with the current coroner?" she asked Gabe.

"Nothing, if you think it's okay to eat a messy sandwich on the autopsy table."

Dalida looked a little queasy. "Surely not while there's a body on it."

"No, not..." Gabe turned and raised his eyebrow at Ollie. Ollie shrugged. "Well, not that I've ever seen, at least."

"This town continues to astound me," she murmured.

"Congratulations, Ollie, I think it's fantastic." I smiled at him. "But it doesn't solve our problem," I pointed out.

The group grew quiet as everyone tried to come up with a solution.

"So, I've got one. We have twenty-six other matching—more or less—bottles," Angie said. Looking around, she raised her eyebrow. "Why can't we just say it's part of the set and it's our bottle? No one else is going to make a claim to it."

Pepper leaned her chin in her hand and tapped her face with her index finger. "She's got a point. We can just submit a claim, say the bottle is ours, and we want it back. He wasn't whacked on the head with a bottle. That should be simple enough, and it has the side benefit of not being illegal."

"It's still a little illegal, but not too bad. So who makes a claim?" Ollie asked.

"It is not illegal—she's the mystic. The bottle is

meant for Fortuna to open. Fortuna owns the art shop, and she's displaying the empty bottles in the back studio," Angie said, turning toward me. "Every one of your students has seen them. You can claim it was here, and someone stole it. Easy peasy. No one's going to remember whether it was twenty-six or twenty-seven bottles on the shelf, right?"

I groaned as I sat back in my chair. "If I do this, your father's going to think I had something to do with Noble."

"What, the murder?" Angie rolled her eyes and waved her hand at the concern. "You didn't even know Conrad Noble."

Gabe looked at Angie. "Before your dad worked with Fortuna, he was a bit suspicious of her."

"So what? The woman's a telepath. She'll know what to say and what not to say. Besides, my dad knows that she's my sister. She'll walk in, fill out the paperwork, get the bottle, and we'll be done with this. You guys are way too paranoid." Angie's greyhound edged his head into her lap and sighed. "This is the simplest way to get the bottle. No one risks going to jail, no one has to steal anything, no one risks their political career. I'm telling you. Easy."

* * *

"You own the bottle," Chief Clutterbuck said, his voice dripping with suspicion.

"Yes, sir," I answered cheerfully. "It's one of a set of twenty-seven. Ollie had mentioned the bottle in poor Mr. Noble's hand when he and Pepper came over. It sounded remarkably similar to one I had on a shelf in the back of my studio. I went and checked, and it wasn't there anymore." The chief blinked back at me, his face echoing the disbelief I felt pouring off him and the detective with him. "So, it must be my bottle." I pushed the claim paper forward. "I'd like it back, please."

Detective Beau Conroe stood behind Chief Clutterbuck, listening to our conversation. He swung his handcuffs around his finger, an amused look on his face. "That bottle is evidence, Ms. Delphi," Beulah Conroe's son told me over Clutterbuck's shoulder. "We can't just hand it over to you on your say-so, first."

"Second, how do we know it's even yours?" Chief Clutterbuck added.

"I think that was actually my point, chief," Conroe told his boss.

Clutterbuck turned and glared at him.

Detective Conroe cleared his throat and stepped back. "You said it much better, sir."

Clutterbuck stared at the detective for a few more seconds, then turned back to face me.

"I brought a picture of all twenty-seven bottles," I said, sliding a doctored photo next to the form. Since the image wasn't really evidence of anything, Ollie felt comfortable manipulating it to place the twenty-seventh bottle on the shelf next to the others. "See, right there," I pointed, tapping the corner.

I could feel that neither believed me.

I could also feel that neither could find any reason I would lie.

"Detective Conroe is right about one thing," Chief Clutterbuck said as he reached forward to gather up the photo and the form. "Conrad Noble had your bottle in a dead man's grip. Literally. It was the last thing he touched in the world, and we're going to have to keep it for evidence until we solve this case."

"Evidence of what?" I asked incredulously. "The bottle didn't shoot him in the head."

A wave of stormy anger passed over Chief Clutterbuck's face. "Now you listen here," he started, lowering his voice so the other officers milling about couldn't hear him. "You may think just because you're another daughter of that horrible Karen White that you have some kind of special standing here, but you don't. I know that my daughter's moved in with you, but I don't know what game you're playing." He shifted closer as his eyes narrowed. "What I can tell you is that your mother is one of the most conniving women God Almighty made the mistake of creating. You may be like my daughter, but you could also be like your mother. And I don't trust you."

At another time, I probably would have been angry at the baseless accusations. This wasn't another time, though, and my heart went out to him. I could feel Terrance Clutterbuck was desperately worried about his daughter. Her ties to Dalida and me were things he hadn't counted on, and he didn't understand. The chief wanted to believe, as she did, that we were three sisters who'd found one another. That we were all victims of my mother.

But he didn't know if he could trust Dalida or me.

He knew he couldn't trust Karen.

And all he knew for sure was that we'd stolen away his daughter.

"Then work with me," I told the chief, the idea coming before I had much chance to think it through. "You know that I've solved cases before, and you and I have worked together before. Reluctantly, I'll admit. You know some of what I can do."

"I still don't know that I believe all that psychic hokum," he answered gruffly.

"Well, you don't have to. You can pretend that you do, and we'll get to know one another," I told him with a soft smile. "Maybe if you get to know me, you'll see that I care about Angie, and I would never do anything to hurt her. If you and I get along? I know it would make her happy."

He winced at my assumption. "And what do you get out of this?"

"I get to know my sister's father, and I get my bottle back." I held out my hand. "What do you say?"

Chief Clutterbuck was a storm of confusion. Over the year or so I'd lived in Mystic's End, I realized what a complicated man he was. Corrupt, yes. Politically savvy? For sure. But right now, I remembered things he didn't remember anymore. I remembered he could be a good man, and it made me sad that my mother wiped his memory and made it so he couldn't.

With all the knowledge of magic (and of me) that he had learned gone, we were starting over.

"There's something about you, Ms. Delphi. My brain says I shouldn't trust you, but my gut says I can." Clutterbuck slowly reached his hand forward and shook mine. "All right, you've got yourself a deal. You help me solve this case, and I'll get you your bottle back." He clutched my hand tight and tugged it aggressively. "But if I find out you have anything to do with Conrad Noble's murder, or you're playing me, I'll throw you in the cell next to your mother. You got me?"

I gulped, then nodded.

FOUR

I shivered in the cool evening breeze. For one moment, I contemplated ringing the outrageously loud doorbell to Martin's huge house, but the ostentatious gongs made me cringe. As usual, I knocked on the thick door and waited. Since my boyfriend was a vampire with super-senses, he would hear it.

Instead of Chris, Martin's Aunt Addie answered the door.

"Fortuna! Sweetheart, you're a little late. Jeeves came up from the basement hours ago." Stepping back, she waved me in. Addie was in her sixties, and she pulled her long gray hair back in a bun. "He's on the veranda with Martin and Angie. They're all quite excited about the last bottle. I am, too, of course."

"I figured you would be. I really hope that this is the last thing we need to get your sister out of that rock." I stepped in, and she closed the door behind me. "I wasn't coming to see Chris for breakfast or anything. Well, his breakfast. Martin and Angie invited me over for dinner, so I think I'm on time."

"Oh, that's right, he wants to go by Chris now, doesn't he," Aunt Addie murmured. "I've been calling that vampire Jeeves for so many years, I don't know that I'll ever get used to calling him Chris. He doesn't even seem like a Chris. He seems like a Jeeves. Anyway, do you really think we will get Anna out of her prison once the bottle is uncorked?"

"I talked to Miss Bessie and Mary and Anna." Aunt Addie led me down a hallway lit by faintly glowing lamps, toward the back of the house. "Miss Bessie is absolutely sure there are only twenty-seven bottles, and we are pretty sure the bottle found this afternoon is that last one."

"Do we know who's in it?"

"There is no record of who's captured in the bottles," I replied. We stopped just before the glass door leading to the backyard. Clearly intending to finish this conversation before she brought me out, Aunt Addie turned to face me and stared expectantly. "Mostly, it seems like the ghosts were nothing more than descendants that held some level of magical power. Once we talked to them all, there's no evidence of some town conspiracy the way Miss Bessie was told."

"Except with my sister." Aunt Addie gave me a stern look.

"Yes, well, your sister was a different story altogether, unfortunately."

"I always knew that Anna would get herself in trouble," the older woman said, shaking her head. "My sister could tumble into a rock after passing a warning sign about the hard place." Addie's voice was soft, but her eyes were sharp and judgmental. "At least she had fun before stumbling into the consequences of her actions. I haven't had one whit of fun since she did it, but that's fine." Aunt Addie gave a long-suffering sigh. "My sister and her predicaments."

"I think Anna is very aware of what a great sister you are and what a fantastic son she has." I smiled.

"Don't try to soothe my hurt feelings, Fortuna." Aunt Addie shook her finger good-naturedly at me. "I've been saving up a lecture for my sister for a few decades now. I'm keeping all this steam, thank you very much." She reached out and took my hand in both of hers, squeezing affectionately. "We're fortunate to have found you." Then she winked. "The vampire especially."

I blushed.

"Go on, go with your friends and your sister," Addie said, opening the back door and waving me out into the night. "It's a lovely evening; you don't need to be jabber-jawing with an old woman inside when there's wine and food under the stars. Oh, to be young again." She winked.

As I walked out, I thought about how much calmer everyone was. It was almost as if everyone involved could sense the end was near, the issue almost solved, the world almost righted. Since my mother was in jail, the threat had passed—that was probably the reason everyone was so nonchalant about the last bottle and about freeing Anna.

That must be it.

* * *

"Do you really think this is wise?" Chris asked as I finished telling everyone about my conversation with Chief Clutterbuck. "The man clearly doesn't trust you, and I don't know that becoming the unofficial police psychic is a good way to get him to do so."

"I think we need that bottle. And Angie's father is so confused." I turned from the sparkling view on the veranda. "I mean, I don't think he even knows that he's confused, but he is. Our mother punched a hole in his memories. His ability to tie this all together...The facts in his head are like Swiss cheese. She removed some recollections but not others, some knowledge but not other knowledge." I took a sip of wine. "It was a messy spell. Which stands to reason, considering she was in a panic and just reacted."

"I wouldn't worry about it. Dad'll come around eventually," Angie shrugged. My sister held a glass of sparkling water. "He just has to work it all out in his own time. Hey, he doesn't want to kill Martin anymore. That's progress."

"Speaking of progress," Martin said, turning toward me. "We only have two dogs left to re-home. And to be honest, I'm not sure they're going anywhere. Hoyt is quite attached to them. He may adopt them both."

"Hoyt?" I asked, surprised. When I first met Hoyt Abernathy, I was sure the guy was an animal abuser. Turns out he had a pretty evil father, and once dear old dad was hauled off to jail? Hoyt made a lot of progress as a human being. I turned toward Angie. "Hoyt really seems to have turned his life around since the two of you pushed Spike down the stairs and stuffed him in a wall."

"You're never going to let me forget that, are you?" Angie said, sticking her tongue out.

"Yeah, no, probably not." I stuck my tongue out at her.

"Wow. Fortuna, did you just make a joke?" Angie stared at me, eyes wide. Turning to Martin, she tilted her head. "How could you have ever thought about dating Fortuna? I mean, seriously?"

Martin shifted on the outdoor sofa and coughed uncomfortably. "Would anyone like more wine? Sparkling soda, perhaps?"

"Isn't he smooth?" Angie winked at me.

"How's the track doing now with all the dogs gone?" I asked Martin, changing the subject from Angie's manslaughter past and the dates I had with Martin.

"Well, it's not really a track anymore." Martin leaned forward, looking grateful the subject had changed to business. Angie walked over, sat next to him, and tucked her feet up beneath her. "But I make more than enough income from the restaurants, shops, and the casino. We'll be fine. Hoyt is actually converting his kennel into an animal shelter. Not sure if you heard."

"Wow, that's outstanding. I'll have to give Hoyt a ring. One of my closest friends down in Texas runs an animal shelter. Maybe she can give him some pointers. Or just be there if he needs advice."

Chris sat down next to me and put his arm around me. I leaned in casually.

"We're going to start on construction in a few months to get rid of all the greyhound racing stuff. Well, other than the animal shelter, obviously. Martin's building a water park instead," Angie said with excitement. Martin smiled at her, and in that smile, I saw Martin's decision to build a water park had a lot to do with my sister's desire for one.

"Won't that be weird? A water park next to a strip club?" I asked her.

"What strip club?" Angie asked innocently.

"The one that's at the south end of the property?"

"I'm sure I don't know what you're talking about," my sister chirped. "There is no strip club at the south end of the property. You must be mistaken."

Chris and I shared a knowing glance. Apparently, a water park's appearance wasn't the only change my sister's desires had brought about at the entertainment complex.

"This all just seems so weird," I said more to myself than anything else.

Martin's face tensed. "What's weird?"

"This." I gestured toward the canapés on the glass table between us, at the view over the city, then toward the meticulous table set for dinner. "All of us sitting on the patio, relaxing, talking about random things. It feels...I don't know, it feels wrong somehow."

"My father is off in Las Vegas, licking his wounds, Karen is rotting in a jail cell. The curse is almost gone, my mother is almost freed, and whoever is in that last bottle will be uncorked within days, I'm sure." Martin glanced at Chris and Angie as if to seek reassurance his statements were accurate. "If there's nothing we can do right now, why is it so wrong that we just sit back, relax, and have a nice evening together?"

"I told you she wouldn't be able to relax," Angie told Martin.

"It just doesn't feel right not to be working towards something."

"You are working towards something," Angie said sarcastically. "You're working on your relationship with him. And with me. Tomorrow, you'll work with the police department and figure out who killed Conrad Noble. You'll get the bottle, you'll uncork it, we will go get Anna out of that rock, and she'll absolutely adore that I'm dating her son."

Martin smiled.

"Fortuna and I have had plenty of time to spend with one another," Chris replied quietly, his arm tighter around my shoulder. "Remember, she's carried much of this on her shoulders alone for over a year. Slowing down, not having multiple things to worry about? This is new for her. Cut her some slack."

"I know it's still unfinished," Martin agreed, nodding. "It's hard for me, too, knowing my mother is stuck in that hole. But I've gotten to talk to her through you, and she seems all right. Since Karen's arrested, I know she's safe from attack. It's easier to have patience." His face fell and grew serious. "Remember, I've been working toward this a very long time."

"I know, and I don't mean to be Debbie Downer," I said with a sigh. "Everything just feels so normal now. Gabe and Dalida are dating, his private investigations business is doing great. You two are dating. Heck, I think even Spike and Plum are dating. Or at least he's trying to. Pepper and Ollie are doing great; Ollie's running to be county coroner. Pepper's doing great at the paper. She just got promoted. Did you know that?"

"Of course, we knew that. She's told everyone she knows," Angie said.

"At least twice," Martin agreed.

I sighed. "I'm ridiculous. I think I said great five times. Everything's great. I should just be happy."

And maybe I was. Yet I couldn't help but feel everything was about to change and it was making me uneasy. As soon as we broke the curse, the ghosts would likely move on to wherever spirits move on to. Martin and his mother might move back to Las Vegas, taking Angie with them.

Who is the mystic of Mystic's End once we break the curse? Did I discover who I was just to lose everything that made me...

Well, me?

* * *

The lights of Mystic's End twinkled as I stood at the rail overlooking the town that was now my home. Even though it was dark, I could feel the surrounding mountains. The forests that covered them came alive at night with energy.

"Did you want to be alone?" Chris asked politely.

I turned and looked at the vampire. Dressed in the white shirt and black slacks of his driver's uniform, he seemed allergic to color. I couldn't ever recall seeing him in anything other than black and white. His dark eyes, always so intense, held mine without wavering. A boyish grin played on his pale face, his red lips striking when he smiled.

"I'm used to being alone," I said without answering his question. "Now, I'm rarely alone."

"Are you having trouble getting used to it?"

"Having people around?"

"People, sisters, ghosts, vampires." He stepped forward and gently put his arms around me. Vampires were so powerful. They felt like walking marble statues encased in vinyl. "Lots of people in the world would love to have half of the family that you now have."

"I seem ungrateful, don't I?" I sighed and leaned into him, snaking my arm up so I could run my fingers through his thick, dark hair. "I don't mean to be. It's a change, and..."

"And?" he asked kindly.

"I'm used to being alone. Now I have two sisters, ghosts coming in and out of my house all hours of the day and night. It's just complicated. And weird. I don't know how to be anybody's sister, you know? Or anyone's girlfriend. And then..."

"There is your mother," he finished for me, hearing the echo of my thoughts before I could make myself say the words.

"She's not really my mother," I told him fiercely, pulling back. His arms held firm.

"She is your history," Chris whispered as he stared into my eyes. "She is your origin story, as they say. Where we come from? We all carry that with us no matter what we become. It's always here." He tapped his chest where his heart would be if he were human. "The things we've experienced, the things we know, the choices we've made. That your mother is not a good person doesn't change who you are. But it is something you're going to have to process through."

It was almost impossible for me to not feel the emotion surging through him. His energy enveloped me, and each thought whispered. There was worry that I wasn't okay, anger that I had to deal with this, resentment that Karen had toyed with me. Those feelings competed with gratitude that she'd given me life and her misdeeds had brought me here to him. Chris's conflict regarding my mother was almost as intense as my own.

"I know, but not tonight," I told him, leaning my forehead against his shoulder. "Tonight, I want to try to be normal."

"She says as she wraps her arms around her vampire boyfriend," Chris chuckled.

"Stop. You may be the most normal thing in my life."

"Considering your life, my love, I'm not sure that's such a high bar." The tenderness in his voice made me feel like I was melting. He trailed his fingers down my neck and I shivered. "It's true, you know."

"What? That my life isn't normal?" I responded as I pulled away. "I'm well aware my life is not normal; you don't need to remind me, thanks." I pushed him away gently and turned back to look out over the town.

Yes, I totally realized that he called me "my love."

Yes, I get that he was about to make a formal declaration of his feelings.

Why do you think I pulled away and stared at the skyline of Mystic's End at that very moment?

I wasn't sure I was ready to hear it.

Judging by the sigh I heard behind me, Chris was sure I wasn't ready to listen to it.

FIVE

I was uncharacteristically nervous when I walked into the Mystic's End Police Department the following morning. I spent most of my time in this town trying to avoid the police—and Chief Clutterbuck pretty specifically. Now, I was walking in as if it was my first day on the job. Plus, it was the closest I'd been to my mother since the night they arrested her. "Excuse me," I said to a young, fresh-faced officer behind the counter. "I believe Chief Clutterbuck is expecting me?"

The officer made some kind of sound in response. Whether it was an acknowledgment or protest, I couldn't tell. A distinct wave of fear came from the young man as he met my eyes. "You the psychic?"

"I don't call myself that, but I suppose if you're expecting one, I'm probably it," I responded as cheerfully as I could. The officer's thick shoulders rose and fell in an elaborate shrug. An awkward pause. "Yes, Officer, I'm the psychic."

"You can go wait over there," he said, hitching his head toward a long wooden bench. "Chief Clutterbuck will come out and take you back when he has some time." I felt his eyes on me as I walked over and sat down.

Images invaded my mind, and I realized I was seeing a discussion the young man had with his mother before he came to work. "You stay away from that psychic woman," his mother told him sternly, her eyes drilling into him as she removed the half-eaten plate of pancakes. "You know what Reverend Kane says about those people. We have to protect the ghosts now. The whole town, going back years. The entire town is depending on us." The young man promised his mother he would do so.

"Well, at least you're on time," Clutterbuck's voice broke into the mental movie I watched in my mind.

"I'm always on time," I told him, standing up. "Well, actually, that's not really true. But I appreciate you allowing me to help on this case, and

I wanted to make sure I didn't cause you any inconvenience."

Another sound came from the young officer. Clutterbuck's head turned, and he gave the young man a harsh stare. "Officer Corbin, you have something you want to say?"

"No, sir," the young man answered quickly. He paused for a few seconds, his mouth twisting wryly to show he did, in fact, have something to say. "I'm sure you have reasons for doing what you're doing with her." He waved in my direction. "But it's not right. My mama and my church tell me people like her? They ain't right. Besides, she probably can't even do what she claims, anyway."

"Were you not hungry this morning at breakfast, Officer Corbin?" I asked him quietly. "Those pancakes looked fantastic. I can't imagine why you wouldn't finish them after your mother went through all the trouble of making them for you."

The young man's face turned as white as the flour dear old mom used to make his pancakes.

"I'm only here to help, officer." I felt some sympathy for the young men. I realize some people get freaked out by the concept of magic or psychic phenomena. I'd wrestled continuously with the ethics of my ability, how far I should feel comfortable pushing into someone else's mind. For those that couldn't keep me out, the idea that I could get in was no doubt frightening.

But Officer Corbin's reaction seemed more than that. The conversation I overheard in his mind made the hair stand up on the back of my neck. What ghosts could these people possibly think they were protecting? Every spirit I knew in town hung out in my living room. Beulah Conroe's visit bubbled up in my memory.

"If the chief thinks you can be of help, I guess that's what's going to happen. Excuse me," he responded hastily. The young man's color was still flat white, almost as pale as Chris's. He ran his fingers through his shaggy brown hair and glared at me before turning and walking away.

"Some people will not be happy that you're here," Chief Clutterbuck said as we watched the young officer walk away. "I have to tell you, Ms. Delphi, I'm not at all sure I'm happy that you're here." Regret tinged his voice as if he couldn't understand his own decision to welcome me as a consultant on this case. "But you are right about one thing, I do want to get to know my daughter's new sister. And, well," he said, shifting uncomfortably. "This case is giving us a headache."

"Do you have a murder board or something?" I asked him.

"A murder board?" he raised his eyebrow.

"Yeah, like one of those cork boards with the red string and push pins and stuff," I answered, trying to sound like I knew what I was talking about. He continued to stare at me, and his eyebrow did not arch back down. "Do you guys not have those? I see them on TV all the time."

"You watch a lot of 1950s detective shows?"

How did he know?

* * *

"We have an evidence room over here." Chief Clutterbuck led me through the spacious primary room of the department. Passing the waiting area filled with benches, the two of us walked straight toward a pair of elaborate double oak doors. I marveled at them, amazed at how fancy a pair of doors could be in a police station, and wondering why on earth someone had chosen them. Through the threshold was a large room filled with a boardroom-sized table and chairs. Someone had strewn pads of paper and pens about. Most forms were blank. "As you can see, we don't have much."

I scanned the room quickly, hoping to see the witch bottle, but it wasn't there.

On one wall, a long dry-erase board's vast expanse of white screamed how little had been done. Conrad Noble's name and age (47) was written large across the top. GSW as a cause of death. The coroner estimated Councilman Noble was shot at 8:17 in the morning thanks to an ear-witness outside the office building who claimed to have heard the gunshot. His receptionist, Clarissa Beauregard, found him at his desk, dead, at 8:35 a.m.

There were no suspects listed.

"That's it?" I asked. "You don't even have the name of the ear-witness down." I pointed. "It's just listed as 'ear-witness.' Don't you think who the ear-witness is might be necessary to know?"

"I don't think that ear-witness is a suspect, if that's what you're saying," Chief Clutterbuck said as he stepped forward and uncapped a marker. In large letters, he wrote the name Bond Noble. "There, are you happy now?"

I bit my tongue before I popped off with a snide comment about shoddy police work. It's worth it to note that Chief Clutterbuck and I were the only two people in the supposed "evidence room" trying to figure out who killed the councilman. That alone showed shoddy police work, if you ask me—but I didn't think expressing my opinions to Chief Clutterbuck would get me anywhere. It would not get me closer to the witch bottle. "Is Bond Noble any relation to Conrad Noble?" I asked politely.

Chief Clutterbuck nodded. "It's his younger

brother. According to Bond, the two of them had breakfast at the Mystic Diner together. They walked the block and a half to Conrad's office; Bond said goodbye to him on the office building steps and headed back toward his car. As he was walking away, he heard a single gunshot."

"That would mean that whoever shot him was waiting for him in his office."

"Is that a psychic premonition or something?" Chief Clutterbuck asked.

"You can't have a premonition about something that's already happened, but no, it's not. It's logic. Bond would have to be in the building's front and close enough to hear the gunshot." I glanced at the building's image, an arrow pointing to Conrad's window on the second floor. "Conrad Noble would've had to go up the front stairs of the building, get in the secured door, go into the hallway, and then up another flight of stairs. Then he would have to unlock his office, go in, sit down at his desk—all before getting shot, and all before his brother got far enough away from the building to hear it." I turned to Chief Clutterbuck. "Is that even possible?"

"Gunshots are pretty loud," Clutterbuck's responded.

"Did anyone else hear the gunshot?"

The chief shook his head no. "Not that anyone reported, no."

"Wait, did Bond Noble actually call 911 about the gunshot?"

The chief walked over to the table and sifted through some papers. Picking up a yellow one, he skimmed over it. "He called in to report hearing a gunshot at 8:17 a.m." Chief Clutterbuck flipped through a few more sheets of paper. "It looks like Bobby Newsom based the time of death off Bond's 911 call."

I made a face. "Sure, why bother to do an autopsy to establish facts when you can just take readily available ones and make them fit?"

Clutterbuck looked uncomfortable with my observation, but he didn't disagree with me. "Newsom is a county employee. I'm a city police chief. I don't have any authority over how he investigates or how he decides things like this. I have to go off of what I'm handed." He shot me a look that was a textbook example of disgust. "But I can't argue with your point."

"So, where do you want to start?"

"Detective Conroe talked to Bond, but it's clear it wasn't a very long conversation," Chief Clutterbuck said as he leaned against the table. "How much psychic whizzum-a-gig can you do when talking to a fellow? Can you tell if they're lying? Are you able to figure out what they're lying about?"

I shrugged. "It depends on how far I want to go, really. People scream out mentally, and I just sort of pay attention to it as it flies by. Like with your officer out there and his pancakes. Then, there are times when people try to hide things, and I have to go in there and dig them out. I'm less comfortable doing that, to tell you the truth," I admitted to the chief. "But if needed, if it gets to that point, I can do it."

Chief Clutterbuck looked uncomfortable with my confession.

"Anything else you want to know?" I asked.

"You don't think much of me, do you?" he asked out of nowhere.

I blinked, not sure I'd actually heard the question said out loud. "I'm sorry?"

"You don't think much of me," he repeated, and this time I was sure he had actually spoken the words. "I don't know you very well, and the fact that my daughter is now wrapped up in whatever this psychic hokum stuff is...I've given Martin Salvi a wide berth since he came to this town. The man brought money, and he brought jobs, and so I did what I had to do to keep him and his father happy." His face tightened. "Yes, I knew who his father was. And I wasn't happy with some decisions I had to make. But I did it to keep this town safe." Chief Clutterbuck's face softened. "To keep my daughter safe."

"I think you did a really good job, Chief Clutterbuck," I told him sincerely. "Angie was a mess for a lot of reasons, and things with her could've gone terrible really fast. It didn't, because you took care of her."

Chief Clutterbuck looked down as if embarrassed. "She didn't mean for anything to happen to that boy, you know."

"Spike?" I asked. Clutterbuck nodded. "I know. And so does he."

"Wherever he is, I hope he does, God rest his soul," the chief murmured.

"I think this is a strange town with a lot of strange things," I continued leaning forward. "I've done some things I didn't think I would do, to be honest. We can't change the past. We can only change ourselves in the future once we understand the mistakes we've made. I know you're the type of person who does that."

He lifted his head up and looked me in the eye. "Psychic impression?"

"Yeah, let's go with that."

* * *

"Why are you even talking to me?" The man was wearing a red cap over his short-cropped hair, and the red ember of his cigarette glowed to punctuate every sentence he spoke. The smell of tobacco around him was so strong that it was hard for me to breathe. "Shouldn't you be out looking for the person who shot my brother?" Though Conrad was the elder brother by five years, even dead, he looked ten years younger than this perpetual chimney.

"Could you put that out, please?" I asked, waving a hand in front of my face.

"Maybe you should step back five feet, honey," Bond shot back.

"I hardly doubt that would be enough," I muttered.

"Why did you bring a woman here?" Bond asked Chief Clutterbuck.

I swallowed the urge to punch the man in the face.

When we arrived at Bond Noble's home, he didn't invite us in. The small house on the working-class side of town was clean and neatly kept but rundown and in obvious disrepair. Windows were taped with duct tape, paint was peeling. Since he stepped out onto the porch to join us on the walkway, I had no way of knowing what it looked like inside.

"Mr. Noble, we just want to go over your story one more time. Sometimes, with a little distance from the trauma of the event, people can remember things they observed or heard that they may not have told us initially," Chief Clutterbuck explained as he glanced toward Bond's home.

Bond Noble didn't look like he'd experienced any trauma. All I picked up from him was a nervous energy that seemed to have nowhere to go.

"I told everything to that other detective yesterday," Bond waved off the chief's question. "If you have some specific question, just spit it out. Otherwise, I have to plan for my brother's funeral." An image of Conrad Noble's wife, Prunella, flashed in his mind.

"Oh, are you helping Prunella with the arrangements?" I asked as if she and I were acquainted. We weren't. "How is she doing? She must be devastated."

"I don't care about how that woman is doing," Bond said, but he looked away from my eyes. "I have to try to figure out how to explain to our parents that Conrad's been shot. They both have dementia, you know. I don't even know that they'll remember. Or how to get them to the funeral." He threw his cigarette down on the sidewalk, stomped it out, and immediately lit another one up. "So, see, I don't have time for you. Go, do your job. Isn't that what we pay taxes for?"

It was over a full day since his brother had been shot, and yet he still hadn't arranged to give the news to his parents. Something about it struck me as wrong—even if they were both suffering from dementia. It didn't seem right not to let them know what happened to their eldest son.

"I apologize for bothering you, Mr. Noble. Clearly, you have a lot on your mind, and we don't want to take up any more of your time," Chief Clutterbuck said, reaching out and extending his hand. Bond stared at it as if it was some trick, and after more time than was appropriate, shook once. "We'll keep your brother's wife informed of our investigation and will call next time if we need to speak with you again."

"Yeah, yeah, okay, that's fine," he said scornfully, turning away—but not before I'd seen relief in his eyes. With the cigarette still dangling between his lips, he took the stairs two at a time and went back into his house. The door shut with a loud slam, and I distinctly heard the click of locks being turned.

"My police instincts say that he's hiding something," the chief said as we walked back toward his car.

"He was defensive, I can tell you that," I responded. "I didn't dig too deep, but something felt off about him. He was thrilled that we didn't push any further and left."

"Not usually the reaction of loved ones looking to catch a murderer." Chief Clutterbuck opened the passenger door for me and stood back like a gentleman. "In fact, he seemed more annoyed by his brother dying than anything else. Like it was inconveniencing him."

"You're good at reading people," I told the chief as I slid into the car.

"Thank you, Ms. Delphi." Chief Clutterbuck closed the door and walked around the car to the driver's seat. After getting in, buckling up, and starting up the engine, he glanced over at me. "Ever been to a crime scene?"

I wisely decided not to answer.

SIX

Crime scenes are strange.

Not that I'd been to a lot.

The violence that happened, the energy of the moment? It's like it hangs in the air.

I could claim this was a psychic thing, but I don't think it is, really. Knowing what transpired in that room made me see it with suspicious eyes. Unnerved eyes. I felt the significance of it, this place where Conrad Noble's life came to an abrupt end at the hand of another.

Conrad Noble was breathing, seeing, hearing... right in that chair.

The next minute, he wasn't.

The chief broke the silence. "Are you getting anything?" Clutterbuck asked me.

"You mean, like, nauseous or something?" I asked, confused.

"No, I mean like psychic impressions," he responded with a self-righteous glare. "Isn't that why you're here?"

"What are you people doing here?" I jumped, turning to find an outraged blonde woman in a short skirt and thin blouse staring at us with fury in her eyes. Behind her was a door I hadn't spotted. "No one should be in here! The police said!"

"Ma'am, are you Clarissa Beauregard?" Clutterbuck asked the angry woman as he reached into his back pocket for his badge. "My name is Terrance Clutterbuck. I'm the chief of police. This is Fortuna Delphi, she—"

"You're the town psychic!" the woman said excitedly. "Are you here to talk to Conrad's ghost? Did you bring her in to try to speak to him in the great beyond?" Her eyes suddenly filled with tears, and she blinked hard to hide them. "Can you see him? Is he all right?"

"Ma'am, I'm not the town psychic, and I'm not—"

"You kind of are," Clutterbuck said with more humor than I felt was appropriate for a crime scene. "You are here as a psychic consultant, so she's not far off."

"Is he here? Do you see him?" Clarissa asked me urgently.

I looked around, then shook my head. "No, ma'am, I'm sorry. If his spirit was here, it's not here anymore."

"What do you mean? If his spirit was here? They killed him here." The secretary looked at me sharply. "Where else would his ghost go? Don't souls have to leave the body at death?" Her eyes widened again. "Is there a door or something that opens for them to walk through?"

Well, her attitude could turn on a dime.

"We're just here to look at the crime scene, ma'am, and see if there's anything I can pick up on. That's all." I moved toward Conrad Noble's desk and looked down as Clarissa made her way over to Chief Clutterbuck. She was chattering away about something or another, but I tuned her out to study the papers strewn about the desk. "Has anything been moved off the desk? By the police, or by you, Ms. Beauregard?"

The two stopped talking and turned toward me. Clutterbuck glanced down. "Not that I'm aware of."

"I have touched nothing," Clarissa responded. A tiny, itty bitty flicker of contempt crossed her face as she answered. It was enough to surprise me.

"The police told me not to touch anything on his desk, and so I didn't."

I called up the memory of the picture Pepper had shown me. Though I wasn't able to see how many papers were beneath Conrad Noble as he lay prone across his desk, I could tell a folder on the right side of his desk was different. Leaning forward, I stared at it—they had moved it for sure. Not only that, there was a distinct gap in the bloodstain pattern. Right where the tag of the folder was—as if something that was no longer there had blocked the spray.

The folder's label could still be clearly seen through the blood, though.

Someone tagged it Holy Grove Church.

"Was the councilman involved with something going on at Holy Grove?" I asked Clarissa, waving toward the now empty folder. "This folder was right on top."

She studied me in the midmorning light, and I felt her defensiveness spring into the air. With a purposeful stride she headed toward the desk and looked down at the folder. "Well, I'm sure I wouldn't know what that was about." She threw me a glance. "If it was necessary, I imagine Mr. Noble would've told me. But since he didn't, it's likely nothing. Maybe they were making plans to have

someone from the church lead the prayer at the
City Council meeting."

She came up with that guess awfully quickly.

"But, truly, you're the psychic." Clarissa gazed
at me. "Don't you know what the folder is about?"

"It definitely jumped out at me as being
important." I smiled. "Since I am psychic and all.
That's why I asked."

Chief Clutterbuck watched me. His expression
was unreadable, and I felt he was taking great pains
to seem merely curious. Like he wasn't genuinely
marking the conversation at all—but his eyes
bounced back and forth between Clarissa and me.

"I imagine you should ask Reverend Kane,"
Clarissa blurted while reaching toward the folder as
if to snatch it up.

"Please don't touch that," Clutterbuck's voice
stopped her before her hand got halfway to the desk.

"Right, crime scene, sorry about that." She
shrugged, trying to act nonchalant. "I don't want to
bother the two of you, and you clearly have work to
do. Is there anything else I can do for you?"
Internally, Clarissa was screaming at herself to get
out of here before she said something stupid.

Clutterbuck opened his mouth to ask her some
questions, but I caught his eye and shook my head
ever so slightly. "If you could just give us half an

hour to ourselves, Miss Beauregard, we would be much appreciative. Ms. Delphi needs quiet to do her thing," Clutterbuck lied.

"Right, of course. I need to get over to Prunella's, anyway." She waved her hands around, palms up. "That poor woman is just a mess, don't you know. She and Bond both are just shattered over this." Clarissa turned around and grabbed a tote bag, hitching it over her shoulder. Pointing behind Chief Clutterbuck, he stepped out of the way so she could grab her purse off the visitor's chair. "Please make sure you hit the lock on the way out."

* * *

"You sensed something?" Clutterbuck asked once we both saw her leave out the front door of the building.

"Well, yes, but I also found something. This folder," I told him, waving him over. I pointed out the gap in the bloodstain. He agreed it looked as if papers not fully tucked into the folder had covered the tag. "If the police didn't take the papers in this folder, someone did. And there's another thing," I said, pointing to two small empty spaces on the display shelves behind Noble's office chair. "You see those two spaces where there is no dust?

Someone recently moved those two items. Since I don't have any pictures of the crime scene—"

"Here, I have them," the chief responded, pulling out a tablet and tapping the screen. "Here we are."

I stepped beside him and looked down at the exact photos Pepper had shown me on her phone the night before. Behind Conrad Noble's prone head was a round selenite ball. Next to it was an empty space.

"Looks to me like that crystal ball was there," Clutterbuck said as he carefully leaned toward the shelf. "This other space looks like it could have been where that bottle was." He narrowed his eyes and looked at me. "Wait a minute. How long ago did you say that bottle was stolen?"

I felt cold. "Um, I didn't, but it could have been a while ago, I guess. I didn't really notice."

"I actually think you did, and I don't think you said it was a while ago." Clutterbuck's eyes seem to narrow again, so much so it surprised me he could see out of them. "That bottle isn't really yours, is it?"

"No, it's my bottle," I insisted, sugaring the lie with a flavor of truth. "It's imperative I get it back. It's really important."

"So important it may have been taken a while ago. Long enough to have gathered this much dust"—Clutterbuck pointed to the shelf—"and yet you just now realized it was gone after Conrad Noble was shot and killed." He stepped away from the bookcase and crossed his arms. "Ms. Delphi, am I on the outside of an inside joke here?"

"No, sir." I blurted the words before I had a chance to even consider them.

He studied me for the length of time it would've taken to pull out his handcuffs and arrest me. The silence was interminable, and I shifted nervously on my feet, waiting. But Clutterbuck said nothing.

"Look," I said finally, a feeling of frustration getting the best of me. "You're right; there's more going on here than I can tell you. Some of it, honestly, is for your own protection. You've been through things, Chief Clutterbuck, that you don't even remember you've gone through. You know things that you don't realize you know."

"Is that so?" His expression was wary.

"It is," I nodded emphatically. I had hoped my small confession would disarm him just a little, but it seemed to have the opposite effect. Chief Clutterbuck was now downright suspicious of me. And if he was this suspicious of me now, he would likely be even more so later. "There is a part of you that wants to believe me, isn't there?"

Despite his steady demeanor, he couldn't cover his surprise at my comment.

"That part of you that wants to believe me? That's the part of you that remembers who I am, the part that remembers the things you know about me you don't know you know anymore. If that made any sense." Despite the instinct I was fighting to provide an explanation more complicated than that, I was afraid he would push me away. I needed him to trust me.

And I needed that bottle.

"There's been nothing but confusion since you showed up here," Clutterbuck muttered, mostly under his breath. "And I don't know whether you're doing something to me to make me feel like I can trust you, but you're right—my instinct as a cop says you have an agenda. My instinct as a human being says whatever that agenda is, it's not a bad thing, and I should help you."

"So, are you a cop first, or a human being first?" I asked with a half-smile.

He blinked a few times in surprise and stared at me as I waited again for his response. I knew he felt uneasy at the conversation, troubled by his conflicted feelings. But he wasn't conflicted about the answer he gave me.

"I'm a father first," Clutterbuck told me.

* * *

The two of us spent about an hour going over the office. Other than the missing crystal ball and the missing papers in the Holy Grove Church folder, we found nothing else of note.

Conrad Noble seemed a pretty average guy. He didn't have an obscene amount of money, but he wasn't poor. His father had inherited a small amount of money from his father, who'd been a moonshiner. Once prohibition was repealed, Grandfather Noble opened the first bar in Mystic's End. He then sold it (and the distillery business) for a tidy profit.

Conrad had gone to school for accounting. A whiz with numbers, he'd maintained the small family inheritance with some conservative but well-thought-out investments. The accountant made enough to ensure his family lived a comfortable, if modest, life and that he could pursue a career as a local politician.

"There's just nothing about Conrad Noble that seems offensive to anybody," Clutterbuck said with a sigh as he closed Noble's file cabinet. "He was organized, inoffensive, not rich. Hell, I even knew him to broker compromises on the City Council that got everyone to simmer down. Everyone liked him. He didn't drink, he didn't smoke, doesn't seem like he did drugs. I don't see any evidence of gambling debts. "

"Would someone keep evidence of that in their office, though?" I asked Clutterbuck.

The chief chuckled. "Most men keep things in their office they don't want their wife to find."

"You don't have a lot of faith in men, do you?" I asked without thinking.

A dark cloud passed in front of the older man's face. "Considering I was one of those men that betrayed their wives, I suppose I have reason to think most people aren't honest. I wasn't honest." Clutterbuck thought a moment. "You're supposedly the psychic. Do you find that what most people say matches up to what they think?"

"That's not the easiest question to answer."

"Why is that?"

"Because people speak to...make an impression, get a point across. They're attempting to present themselves in a certain way, to organize their thoughts so they can influence others. What they say and what they think are seldom going to match, not completely. It's not usually out of a desire to lie to someone, though."

The more time I spent with Chief Clutterbuck, the more I found I liked him. I liked his bluntness, the way he went straight to the point of a matter. Well, when he wasn't trying to hide something.

Lying, though, didn't seem his natural state. He struck me as someone who knew what he wanted, and he didn't want to compromise. Despite all the things I'd seen him do that were ethically gray (to be polite about it), I could feel in him a profound respect for right and wrong.

Seeing all this, feeling it...

It made what my mother did to him even worse.

My mother made Terrance Clutterbuck cynical. He'd loved his wife, adored her, and he blew up his life for a mistake I suspect he had no control over making. Because he couldn't understand how he did what he did, he went through life assuming the worst of everyone—because he had believed he was a good man. Once.

And then he made a mistake and destroyed the woman he loved.

"Well, you have a cotton candy way of looking at people, Ms. Delphi. Toughen up for the next few days," Clutterbuck said, pointing at the folder. "Because those items were in this office when we came to get Mr. Noble and take him. Someone came in after and took a crystal ball and some church papers." He looked me in the eye. "I also suspect that Clarissa woman just lied to our face about those papers. And if I'm worth my salt as a lawman, she's probably not going to be the last person to lie to our face."

"She seemed defensive. Like she was hiding something. Not at first, though. As we talked, it got worse. I know she lied about Bond being shattered," I agreed. "He didn't seem bothered by his brother dying."

"No, he didn't, did he?" Chief Clutterbuck contemplated the situation as he stared up at the ceiling. "Clarissa helped us out in one respect."

"Oh?" I asked.

"She let us know that Bond and Prunella may be together. Bond said as much himself," Clutterbuck mused as he looked down at me. "If Clarissa went straight over there, well..." He smiled mischievously. "That'd be an interesting get-together to have, wouldn't you say?"

Interesting is one way to put it.

The chief snapped a few pictures of the crime scene with the tablet to document the folder on the desk and the missing knick-knacks on the shelves. "Okay, let's lock it up and see if the widow Noble is expressing any level of remorse over her husband's untimely demise."

SEVEN

In the car with Chief Clutterbuck, I sat with my arms crossed. Spring in Arkansas was beautiful, but there were days the chill in the air would insinuate itself, reminding everyone that winter wasn't that far gone.

On the one hand, Chris's observation this could be a bad idea might be right. I was going through an awful lot of trouble to cajole my way into the evidence room when it would be faster and easier to simply break into the evidence room. Sure, okay, highly illegal—but infinitely easier. The only time Clutterbuck and I had worked together was when the town was magically poisoned—long story—and he didn't exactly appreciate my talents.

On the other hand, he knew about this town's history from a side I'd never had access to.

The historically corrupt side.

"What do you know about the Holy Grove Church?" I asked him as we drove through town toward Conrad Noble's home.

"Are you asking me about the church's beliefs or about Reverend Dexter Kane?"

"Both, I guess," I told him after thinking about it. "Between the gambling and owning racing dogs and stuff, he just doesn't really strike me like a man of God, you know?"

"Your mother—"

"She's not my mother," I responded automatically.

"Okay, your birth mother," Clutterbuck corrected apologetically. "She and Reverend Kane were real close years ago. I always used to see the two of them—thick as thieves—after the services. Later, when Martin showed up to wash the town in his father's money, I figured they had sent her forward to lay the groundwork."

I frowned. "I thought they only built the track five years ago."

"It takes a long time to pull a project like that together," he said. "Land was being bought, surveying was being done." He paused. "Politicians being purchased. Palms greased. You know, the usual."

"What would the Reverend of a local church have to do with any of that?"

"You'd have to ask them. All I know is they seemed pretty close—maybe too close—for a preacher and a mobster's girlfriend. Not a pair you would normally see chumming around with one another." He paused. "The town definitely noticed."

I had a few interactions with Dexter Kane since I'd moved to Mystic's End. Some routine—he owned Gideon, my greyhound, before I bought him (and put an end to his racing career). I paid well over the going rate thanks to my attachment to the hound, and Dexter Kane was pleased with his profit.

Which was so substantial, I winced at the memory.

But other interactions left me with questions. I hadn't been open more than a few months when Dexter Kane visited my shop to commission a picture for a funeral, a portrait of the recently deceased Hugh Maddox. Despite his parishioner passing away, the Reverend made exceedingly skeevy comments during the transaction.

Going over the memory in my mind, though, his misogynistic comments were not what stood out.

What stood out was Reverend Dexter Kane's shock when he came face to face with my selenite crystal ball. I kept it on the display table at the front of the shop. Patrons walking in could miss it, but when stepping out of the store? It was impossible not to see. At first, it seemed to unnerve him. He stopped stock-still and stared at it.

Then he whirled on me to ask if it was for sale. When I refused to sell it, a flash of ferocious anger crossed his face. It was such a brief moment I remember questioning whether I saw it at all.

He'd never mentioned it again, and so I'd forgotten about it until now.

"Why would Dexter Kane be interested in a selenite crystal ball?" I murmured.

"Kane was interested in Conrad Noble's missing crystal ball?" Clutterbuck asked.

"No. I have one at the shop. They're not exactly uncommon. Since my shop's name is the Mystic Moon Gallery, I keep it upfront as a representation of the moon." I related the interaction I had with Reverend Kane from a year ago. "It just seems weird to me he would have such an intense reaction to seeing mine. Here we are a year later, and another crystal ball is missing from a crime scene where papers on the Holy Grove Church are gone, too. That seems...odd, don't you think?"

Chief Clutterbuck looked uncomfortable as he

pulled in to a house I didn't recognize. "Your questions are making this sound like a conspiracy, Ms. Delphi." He turned off the car and shifted his body to face me. "You're the psychic. Are you getting any impressions that there is more going on here?"

"More than what?" I asked him with a sarcastic chuckle. "They shot a City Councilman point blank in the head. A witch bottle, and a selenite crystal ball were at the crime scene. The crystal ball has disappeared from the secured crime scene. Paper referencing the local church has also disappeared from that same scene, but the witch bottle is locked up in evidence. I don't think I need to get impressions, Chief Clutterbuck. Something's clearly going on here."

The chief's dark eyes stared at me with unnerving intensity. "What, pray tell, is a witch bottle?"

Just as I realized I'd stupidly said too much, there was a knock on the driver's window.

* * *

"What are you two doing here?" Detective Conroe asked as we stepped out of the car.

"I venture a guess we're doing the same thing as

you," Clutterbuck answered. "Investigating a murder."

"Am I being taken off the case, sir?" Conroe asked his boss stiffly.

"Did I say that?" the chief deadpanned in response. Detective Beau Conroe, son of the Holy Grove Church's own Grace Gang member Beulah Conroe, gave Clutterbuck a fierce glare. Chief Clutterbuck stared down that glare without even flinching. "Did you have something else you wanted to say, Detective?"

"I don't enjoy having my work questioned."

"Did I ask you questions? Seems to me you're the one that started off with questions, son."

I couldn't understand the intense hostility I sensed between the two men. Beau Conroe stared at Terrance Clutterbuck with a towering fury and startling resentment. It was just barely staying contained below the surface.

Clutterbuck was cool as a cucumber as he stared the younger man in the eye, but his dislike was extreme.

A younger man, by the way, immensely distressed the two of us were here.

The detective glanced at me. "What is she doing here?"

"I sent out a memo that Fortuna was going to be consulting on this case. In that memo, I also mentioned that I'd be taking a more active role because Conrad Noble was a City Councilman. Maybe you should read alert information a little more often, Conroe." Clutterbuck gestured toward Beau Conroe's cell phone. "You seem to be a bit out of the loop."

Conroe wanted to sneer, but I sensed him swallowing anger. "Sorry, boss," he said in a tone that didn't sound sorry at all. "I'm well aware that the murder of a local politician is a bit higher profile. Been working hard to uncover leads." He was talking to himself in his head, telling himself to stay calm. Not to attack the chief. "Wouldn't want the mayor to get her panties in a twist."

I hated that expression.

"Do you have any leads?" Clutterbuck asked politely.

"Not yet."

He was lying.

"Well, Fortuna and I found something at Noble's office." Clutterbuck didn't elaborate.

"You planning on sharing it?"

Chief Clutterbuck wasn't particularly fond of Beau Conroe, and Beau wasn't exactly a fan of the chief. Even so, Beau Conroe's anger and fury seemed vastly out of proportion to the situation. I'd never been impressed with Conroe, but I'd sensed nothing in him like what I was sensing now.

"It'll be in the next memo," Clutterbuck told him. "Why don't you go visit the coroner and see if he's got any more information? Fortuna and I will handle interviewing these folks again."

"Again?" the detective asked, startled.

"Well, I assume you've interviewed them already." The chief looked at him oddly. "Conrad Noble's been dead for a full day. It would practically be a dereliction of duty if you hadn't spoken to them yet." Chief Clutterbuck crossed his arms. "Speaking of which, after you talk to the coroner, maybe you should head up to your desk and catch up on your paperwork. I didn't find any notes on those interviews in the case room."

He thinks he's so smart, Conroe thought to himself. *He has no clue what's going on here. He better be helping her get her mother to pony up with the cash for the church. If he's not, the same thing will happen to him.*

"Absolutely, sir, I'll get right on that," Conroe said, nodding once and turning to head back to his car. At least she can't read my mind, he thought to himself. I barely looked her in the eye. Nope, as long as I don't look her in the eye, I'm fine.

I smiled. Whoever's giving him advice on how to deal with a telepath has it super wrong.

Which might be useful.

Since I was now sure Beau Conroe was square

in the middle of the conspiracy we were trying to unravel.

If not the actual murderer.

* * *

"Hold up," I said as Clutterbuck turned toward the front door. He stopped and turned back toward me, his eyebrow raised. "Do you normally have that much animosity between you and the officers that work for you?"

"Beau Conroe is not an officer; he's a detective," Clutterbuck corrected me.

"Oh, for goodness' sake, you guys and your titles," I snapped. "You know exactly what I mean."

"Yes, but I was hoping to avoid this conversation standing in front of a dead man's house. No, Ms. Delphi, I rarely have that much animosity between the detectives on the police force and me. I also don't normally ask psychics to consult on cases, and a City Councilman doesn't normally get shot in the head." His gaze was steady and never shifted. "Whatever you may think of this town, what's happening here is not normal. And I well know it."

"You think Beau Conroe might've had something to do with Conrad Noble's murder?" I asked.

"No, I don't think he killed Noble."

Clutterbuck tilted his head. "But I don't think it's outside the realm of possibility, either. Something strange has been going on since your mother wound up in jail. Secret meetings at the church, strange looks as people come and go from the police station. Things I...things I can't explain."

That piqued my interest. "What things?"

The chief looked around—I assume to make sure no one was within hearing distance—and then leaned closer. "Beau Conroe and your birth mother were seen leaving the church at two o'clock in the morning. Monday night, Tuesday morning. The day before someone shot Conrad Noble."

I blinked. "But she's in jail."

"I'm well aware of that, Ms. Delphi. That's what makes it so odd." He gave me a look that suggested a complicated emotional response to my observation. "I checked the security footage. She appeared to be sleeping in her cell at two o'clock in the morning. I saw no one take her out of her cell, never saw her in the hallway. Didn't see her go through any door. There are cameras all over the Mystic's End Police Department. There's not a single corner of that place uncovered."

"Who saw them there?" I asked him. "At the church, I mean."

Clutterbuck tensed. "It's not important."

"Maybe it is." His reaction suggested it could be

Angie, but I talked to her last night. If she'd seen our birth mother out walking the town, she absolutely would have mentioned it to all of us. There's no way she would keep something like that to herself. Besides, Angie Laroux going to a church? Not likely. She couldn't run fast enough in her high heels to avoid the lightning bolts.

"I'm not ready to tell you," he said, his discomfort clear. "Like I said, things are going on I can't explain. You're the only one I know..." He crossed his arms and frowned. "Look, like I said, something tells me I could trust you. But I'm not sure I trust myself right now. And so I'm not going to tell you. Not yet."

Whoever told him about my birth mother and Beau Conroe...It was like the person rattled him.

I pressed psychically, but he was practiced at hiding his emotions and thoughts. Disciplined. I fought the desire to dive headlong into his third eye like it was a summer's day, and he was a swimming hole. I wasn't entirely sure someone as observant as he wouldn't notice. Especially since he knew what I was.

He already didn't trust me. If I made that mistrust worse...

No, I had to play it the way he wanted to play it.

"Okay, so let's take this a different way—did you

talk to Beau Conroe about someone seeing him? Did you ask if he took Karen White out of her jail cell and to church for some weird small town reason?"

"I did not," he responded, relieved that I had stopped asking about his informant.

"Then why is he so angry at you?"

He thought about it for a moment, trying to figure it out. Finally, he shrugged. "My suspicion is that he is some part of whatever this conspiracy is, and he doesn't like that I'm sticking my nose in. I have done nothing to him at work that would cause him to be so angry at me. It makes little sense. There has to be something he's not saying."

"Oh, there was a lot he wasn't saying," I muttered.

"You heard his thoughts." It was a question more than a statement.

"I did. For some reason, Beau thought if he didn't look me in the eye, I wouldn't be able to do it." I smirked. "He was wrong. He also thought that you had no clue what was going on here. He's angry that my mother isn't supporting the church financially. He's hoping that you're with me to help me do what she wants to do, I think. But he's also worried we'll find out something he doesn't want us to know. What, though, I'm not sure."

"Karen donates money to the church? So she

has something to do with this." Clutterbuck sounded more resigned than surprised.

"I don't know. I wish I could tell you definitively, but I don't know. I think it's probably time for me to share something with you, though." I told him about Beulah Conroe's visit. His eyes widened with shock. "So, you see, you may not be wrong about Beau Conroe being involved with this. Though there's nothing right now that unambiguously, for sure, ties Conrad Noble's death in with whatever is going on with the church. Not for sure." I shrugged again. "But if the two things aren't tied together? That would be an enormous coincidence. The last thought I picked up on was that if you're not helping me, the same thing will happen to you."

"The same thing? That happened to Conrad?" Clutterbuck asked.

"I don't know, that's all he said. Well, thought."

We stood in silence in the late morning sun as the words we'd spoken between us hung there. Both Clutterbuck and I kept secrets from one another, but we'd opened up a little and built a bit of trust.

The problem. By doing that?

We also opened a can of worms and spilled them all over the floor.

EIGHT

Prunella Noble—I assumed—threw open the door moments after Chief Clutterbuck rapped three times in quick succession. The moment she saw the tall man standing on her porch, she froze in shock, then spat, "What are you doing here?" After a moment of silence that didn't last long enough for Clutterbuck to have taken a breath in preparation to answer, she repeated the question. "What are you doing here? Why are you here? Why have you come?"

The chief tried to smile at her. "Mrs. Noble, Ms. Delphi, and I—"

"Delphi!" Prunella Noble looked like she was choking on her tongue, her eyes bugging out as they worked hard to look at me without looking at me.

She took great pains to avoid looking me directly in the eye. "A Delphi! She's a Delphi? Why would you bring a Delphi to this house? How dare you!"

The chief looked confused at the question and the issue with my last name. "Ma'am, I'm not precisely sure what you mean but—"

"Surely, Mr. Clutterbuck, you know that woman's in league with the devil." Tallulah Abernathy, Hoyt Abernathy's grandmother, stepped around the (presumably) grieving widow. Flinging her arm out, she swept Prunella back. "You can't bring one of the devil women in here with a grieving widow. She might call up poor Conrad's ghost, and then where would we be? Or she'll do what she usually does," the woman sneered. "Try to have some innocent soul thrown in jail."

The door hadn't been opened longer than a minute, and I was already sure we weren't getting into the house. Tallulah Abernathy placed her ample girth between the two of us and the hallway. Planting her feet apart, she stared us down defiantly —unafraid to look me in the eye.

"Maybe having me on this case wasn't the smartest decision you've made," I murmured.

"Have all you women just lost your gosh dang minds?" Chief Clutterbuck glowered from beneath the shadowed shelter of the front door overhang. It was a cool spring day, but beads of sweat gathered on his forehead. "You're all acting like you're in some James Patterson novel or something—"

"Laurell Hamilton," I muttered.

"What?" Clutterbuck glared at me.

"I said Laurell K. Hamilton. She writes the Anita Blake series. That's probably more apt because it's got supernatural elements. James Patterson writes—"

"Do you really think this is the time?" Clutterbuck's jaw was so tight I could see his muscles flexing.

"Sorry." I wasn't, really. The last thing I needed was for this to turn into a James Patterson novel.

"A man was shot, and you're all talking about ghosts and trying to pick a fight!" Clutterbuck scrubbed a hand along his jaw with an angry sigh as he looked back at Tallulah Abernathy. "Just what in tarnation is going on in this town?"

"Well, if you'd been attending church, the way you should, you'd know exactly what was going on here, Mr. Clutterbuck," Tallulah responded with a head snap and a judgmental stare. "You wouldn't be running around town with the likes of her, I'll tell you what." Turning toward Prunella, she shook her head. "I swear, everything would be just fine if it wasn't for the men in this town."

"You heard her, copper. We don't need your help. We've got everything under control. Now you get off my porch, and you leave us be," the widow spat as she tried to slam the door. Clutterbuck's hand shot out, and his palm hit against it with a loud smack. "Just what is it you think you're doing!" Prunella barked angrily. "This is my property, and I don't care who you are. You get off my porch!"

"Has everyone in this place gone mad?" Clutterbuck asked again.

Bond Noble raced into the hallway, his eyes wide. "What's going on here, Prunella?"

"This stupid man and his harlot won't leave!" Tallulah told him.

"Harlot!" I barked, insulted. And, to tell you the truth, a little grossed out. Terrance Clutterbuck was the father of my sister, after all. "Now, you wait just a minute!"

"Blood devil harlot!" she hissed while staring at my chin. "You're a heretic! Blood devil harlot!"

I paused. Did she think I was actually a vampire or was that just an insult because I was dating a vampire?

"Get out! You can't come in anyway! You weren't invited!" Prunella screamed.

Chief Clutterbuck's hand was at least ten inches inside the door frame, so I didn't think she was talking about him. Maybe she really did think I was a vampire, or they had grown so used to seeing Chris walk in the daylight thanks to Karen's magic they assumed all vampires could. If they knew he was a vampire. Which I was pretty sure they did, at least at the church.

I reached forward to see if I could slip my arm inside.

A sharp and sudden torrent of air flew from the door and straight toward me. The air smelled electrified, and it slammed me so hard that I felt genuine pain. I stumbled backward, gasping.

"What happened?" Clutterbuck asked, reaching out quickly to study me.

"Warded," I whispered. "The doorway, or the entire house, is warded."

"Awarded what?" he asked, confused.

"Not awarded. Just warded. It's a form of protective magic. Think of it as a magical barrier, like a force field." Prunella and Bond Noble looked horrified that the wards had manifested themselves in front of the chief. Tallulah Abernathy looked wholly satisfied, as if she both expected me to set them off and that they would shove me back. "I can't get in. Someone has set barriers against me. Or people like me."

Clutterbuck looked confounded, as if uncertain whether I was serious. I knew the look. In fact, I knew this look on this man. He'd exhibited it several times throughout the great magical probiotic poisoning of 2020. (Again, long story.) "Wait," he said hesitantly, his eyes cloudy and tense. "I remember. You're a...you're a witch."

"She's a harlot! She's the devil's handmaiden!" Tallulah shouted at Clutterbuck.

With the chief lost in thought, I stood up straight and attempted to stare each in the eye. All —except Tallulah—turned away, wincing. You would've thought I had x-ray vision—though I guess that's (sort of) what they thought I had. Unfortunately, my telepathy was blocked at the door the same as I was, and I could sense nothing.

"We came here to question you about your husband—"

"She's got nothing to say to you," Tallulah told Clutterbuck, and she pushed Prunella back toward Bond. "And if you know what's good for you, you'll get free of that harlot over there, turn around, and forget anything about this case." The old woman's eyes narrowed dangerously. "This ain't got nothing to do with you, and it's for the good of the town. You stay out of our way, now, chief. You hear?"

The door slammed shut.

* * *

"This all sounds ridiculous. You know that, right? Utterly insane," Clutterbuck said after I read him in. What else was I supposed to do?

There was no way to explain the crazy relatives of the dearly departed unless I did.

"I understand." I added nothing else.

If Tallulah hoped Clutterbuck really would just turn around and walk away, the drama on the front porch had precisely the opposite effect. "If I hadn't seen what I saw back at that house with my own eyes, I never would've believed any of this. And you say Angie is a witch, too?"

"She doesn't know how to do a lot," I said as we sat outside the Mystic Diner and picked at our food. The air was still chilly, and the two of us were the only folks in the picnic table area. "She didn't really know she was a witch. But Karen, our mother? She's a witch. Or partial. Not sure, but we inherited the gene, I guess? From her. Angie has some really cool powers, actually."

"Dalida, too," Pepper said as she walked out the diner's back door and slid into a chair at our table without waiting for an invitation. "Angie would make a fortune hiring herself out to doctors. She just touches your hand, and whatever pain you're feeling just goes away. Mental pain, emotional pain, physical pain? Poof, gone."

Clutterbuck stared at her. "You know about all this psychic witch stuff?"

Pepper's face fell. "You don't read my blog?"

Clutterbuck looked as if he'd woken up from a

bad dream to find an even worse reality. "How many of these supposed witch bottles are left?"

"You told him about the witch bottles?" Pepper asked, surprised.

"Well, I wasn't going to tell him about anything. But then he saw me get zapped by wards."

Pepper frowned. "What you mean, he saw you zapped by wards?"

"Conrad and Prunella Noble's house?" I said, grabbing a french fry. "Someone warded the door. Probably the whole house, actually. It's an elemental ward, too. I got knocked in the chest by a gust of wind, and I could smell ozone."

"Ozone?" Pepper made a face. "Why would you smell ozone?"

"I wasn't hit by lightning, but there had to be some somewhere."

"The way you say these things, so matter-of-fact." Clutterbuck shuddered as if a chill had passed through him.

"It is a matter-of-fact to us," I explained, grabbing another fry. "Magic, even magical enemies, and wards. It's all just another day in the life for me, really. I'm kind of used to it."

"Are you a witch, too?" Angie's father asked Pepper.

She shook her head, no. "I've been bit by a vampire, though."

Clutterbuck turned white.

"Oh, shoot, I'm sorry," Pepper said, reaching into my plate and grabbing one of the last remaining fries. "You didn't tell him about the vampires, did you?"

"I hadn't got to them yet, no."

We sat at the table and finished our meal in silence.

Towards the end of the meal, Pepper's eyes traveled back and forth between Clutterbuck and me. Then me and Clutterbuck again. Her foot tapped. Then her finger. The chief was still lost in thought, and Pepper was desperately trying to respect the silence so he could process all he had been told.

Trying.

Eventually, she failed.

"Prunella and Bond deeded the Noble family distillery to the Holy Grove Church," she burst out as if she'd been holding her breath for minutes. Digging into her knapsack, she glanced up. "I'm sorry, chief, I know this whole 'reality differs from what you thought it was' is a lot to take, but I think this has something to do with Conrad's death."

"Why do you think that?" the chief asked her.

"Because it was signed this morning, and if Conrad Noble was alive?"

"It couldn't have happened unless he agreed," I guessed.

She nodded and handed me the papers.

"Hey," Clutterbuck objected. "There is only one law enforcement officer sitting at this table."

"You're 'the man,' chief," Pepper told him with a sunny smile. "I'm a reporter. Independent. The fourth estate. I can't be handing evidence over to the chief of police. My credibility would be shot. My renegade reputation destroyed." She waved at the papers in my hand. "If Fortuna shows you, well, there's nothing I can really do about that, is there?"

Clutterbuck stared at her. "You're a strange woman, Stanford."

Pepper raised her eyebrow. "You just found out she's a witch, and you're calling me strange?"

I continued skimming the papers as Clutterbuck and Pepper bantered back and forth. Suddenly, my eyes fell on a name that made me squint to be sure I read it right. I couldn't understand what this particular attorney would be doing filing these papers. "I know this lawyer," I held up the last page. "Gerard Blatworth."

"Blatworth?" Pepper asked, surprised. "Isn't that Martin's lawyer? The one he got you when Chief Clutterbuck was trying to put you in jail for Hugh Maddox's murder?"

The chief shifted uncomfortably in his chair. "About that, I—"

"Forget it—water under the bridge. But yes, that's the same guy. I would've sworn he worked directly for Martin. Well," I said, leaning back in the chair and thinking. "He worked for the track. Like, the business."

"Which means there's a possibility he worked for Martin's father."

I looked at Chief Clutterbuck and nodded. "Or Karen."

"I think we should go visit Martin. See what he knows about where Blatworth's loyalties lie."

* * *

"This is unexpected," Martin said, giving a start of surprise.

"Daddy!" Angie's smiling, surprised face peeked around the corner. After the verbal greeting, she slipped into her father's arms and gave him a hug. Clutterbuck's expression softened swiftly the moment his daughter touched him, and I could see him taking stock of the changes her nearness brought. "How're you doing, Daddy? Are you being nice to Fortuna?"

"I always said you had a healing touch, Row." He looked down at his daughter as if he'd never quite seen her before. "Fortuna tells me I was right about that."

"I already told you about my powers, sort of," Angie said with a glare in my direction. "What did Fortuna tell you? And why are you calling me Row? You know I hate my birth name." She blushed with embarrassment.

"You shouldn't be. Rowena is a Celtic name, ancient. Its origins aren't entirely certain, but it first appears in Welsh historian Geoffrey of Monmouth's 12th-century *History of Britain's Kings*. Rowena was the daughter of the Saxon chief, Hengist." I smiled warmly at my younger sister. "Kind of appropriate considering who your dad is."

"It just sounds so...so country." She shrugged. "Anyway, what are you guys doing here?"

"We actually have a question for Martin." I handed him the papers Pepper had given me. "These turned up in the investigation into Conrad Noble's death. Prunella—Conrad's wife—and his brother Bond signed over a parcel of land that had been in the Noble family for over a hundred years. They filed the papers just this morning. They were prepared by—"

"Gerard Blatworth," Martin murmured, his eyes scanning documents.

"Does he still work for you?"

Martin looked up. "No. I let him go over a month ago."

"Why?" Chief Clutterbuck asked his future son-in-law. (Oh, come on, we all know it will happen.)

"My father and I had a long talk once...Once we realized..." Martin looked back and forth between Angie and her father as if he was unsure of exactly how much to say.

"I know who you are, son," Clutterbuck told him gruffly. "I knew who you were when you showed up in this town, and I know a lot of what transpired since. I definitely know who your father is. My Row's been telling me about the things you've been doing, taking steps to make the past right. I will not judge you for what you say."

"It's not really that, Sir. It's—"

"He knows Karen's a witch." Martin and Angie turned, their stares curious. "We just came from Prunella's house. It was warded, and I can't get in. Only a witch can set wards, and they were powerful enough they almost knocked me off my feet." Angie bit her lower lip, her eyes darting toward her father. "If there are people from your organization there still helping, my guess is they're helping Karen make some kind of last stand." I gestured toward Clutterbuck. "We have to trust him. He has Karen, he has the last witch bottle, and he may have evidence that shows where the selenite crystal ball went."

"Crystal ball?" Martin asked frowning. "What crystal ball?"

"I feel like we keep getting bits and pieces of this," Clutterbuck interrupted. He stepped forward, ready to take charge. "We're going to spend all our time getting people up to speed." He paused and glanced around. "Call Gabe, Ollie, and Jeeves. Dalida, too—your sister should probably be a part of this. Let's get the whole posse together and go through this once."

"Um, about Jeeves," I began.

"He goes by Chris now, Daddy," Angie told him.

"And he's um...busy for a few hours," Martin added, nodding.

"Busy?" Clutterbuck asked with an eyebrow raised. "If what you say is true, what's more important than this?"

"Oh, for heaven's sake." Pepper rolled her eyes and turned to face the chief of police. "Jeeves is a vampire. He's sleeping somewhere under the ground, away from the sun. He'll be with us at sundown, so let's just set the meeting for then, shall we? In the meantime, go back to the station and get all the evidence from the room. Bring it here."

"I can't bring it here. How would I explain that?"

"To who? You're the chief of police. If you leave it there, you're leaving it in the same building that Karen's in. The room's not warded, is it?" Pepper extended her hands. Her question hung in the air. "No, it's not. But this building is. Bring everything here."

"The bottle, too?" Clutterbuck asked.

"Especially the bottle," Pepper told him. "There's someone in there. Let's make sure she's safe."

NINE

"And now you're caught up," I told Chris as we sat in Martin's large, luxuriously paneled office.

Chris looked as if he understood...but didn't want to. He leaned back in the chair and gently rubbed his fingers together as if attempting to come up with the missing ingredient in lasagna. "Despite all that, no one has the smallest suspicion as to why Conrad Noble was murdered? Or why?"

"Well, we have suspicions. They're not even small," I began hesitantly. I thought I just explained those, but maybe I wasn't clear. "I mean, it probably has something to do with the land Prunella and Bond just signed over to the Holy Grove Church.

And after talking to them this afternoon—or, really, not being able to talk to them—it's clear the land transfer has something to do with Karen, the witch bottle, and the selenite sphere."

"It seems an obvious tie, I suppose." Chris leaned forward, rubbed a thumb and a forefinger down his nose, and looked at me with steady, piercing eyes. His tone didn't sound like he thought anything was obvious. "Maybe that's the problem I'm having with the story so far."

Sorry that our work all day while you were snoozing isn't up to your usual standards, I thought snarkily. I was tired after running around with Clutterbuck all day and a little frustrated at the long wait for Chris to crawl out of bed. After a brief pause, I asked, "What do you mean?"

"It's all too obvious. It's a little too wrapped up in a bow." Chris, my boyfriend, had turned into Jeeves, Martin's bodyguard, in the blink of an eye. All work, laser focus. That it happened before Chris, my boyfriend, had hugged me or asked how my day was?

Probably the reason I was feeling so tart.

Setting it aside, I reminded myself this was where the vampire shined. I could practically feel the gears in his mind turning, clicking everything together, and finding the holes we hadn't had time to plug.

Or, um, spot.

"Which part's too obvious?"

"A crystal ball that you don't know the purpose of stolen from the crime scene," Chris pointed out. "The witch bottle you think you know the purpose of—the very last thing you think you need to break the curse on this town—found in the deceased Mr. Noble's hand." He tilted his head. "Why would the murderer leave the bottle?"

"The murderer actually left both," I pointed out. "The bottle and the ball. They took the bottle into evidence. The ball disappeared from the crime scene later. After they cataloged the crime scene."

"You two ready?" Pepper asked, sticking her head in. Glancing at Chris, she frowned. "How do you do that?"

"Do what?" he responded politely.

"Sundown was, like, 10 minutes ago. How did you manage to come out of a coffin, crawl out of the earth, and still look like an Italian runway model?"

"I've gotten better with practice, I suppose." Chris stood up, and my breath caught—Pepper was right. His black slacks looked freshly pressed, his white shirt was crisp, black leather shoes were shined to a glass-like finish. If I checked the soles of them, I doubted they would show any scuffs. "It also helps that I don't crawl through the earth or sleep in a coffin. You've been watching too many horror movies. I have a secure bedroom downstairs."

"There's a downstairs?" I asked, surprised.

"Well, I guess you two aren't as far along in the relationship as I expected," Pepper quipped.

I blushed.

But she wasn't wrong.

Vampire folklore was quite clear about the... appetites of vampires. The Romany believed the vampire was a sexual entity, with male vampires 'visiting' their widows as their first undead act. The Roma thought the children born of such relationships—which were possible—had unique magical powers to track and destroy vampires attacking the community.

Because clearly what my future needed was "Buffy The Vampire Slayer" as a daughter.

Sure, okay, I'd been doing quite a bit of internet searching and library reading. It's not like there was a "Dear Abby" for how to date a vampire. I'd also watched some British show called "A Discovery of Witches" because it featured an alliance between a witch and a vampire. It...well, let's just say it didn't work out well in the end.

Anyway.

Chris had operated far more like the vampires in "Twilight." He'd been nothing but a perfect gentleman, and we never really talked about the future of our relationship. The vampire never pushed for more than a kiss. He just wasn't the type of guy that let his passions overtake him. My boyfriend was steady. I loved that about him.

"Our relationship, Pepper, is exactly where it needs to be," Chris told her with a confidence that made me swoon. He took two steps and put his arm around me. "Please apologize to the others for the delay. We'll be out in a moment."

Pepper looked like she wanted to say something, but she gave a quick nod and backed out.

"Before we join the others, I want to caution you against running in the most obvious direction without thinking about it." Chris gently turned me to him, his fingers grazing my chin to guide my face upwards. "What you have told me? I understand why it makes sense to you and to the others. But I have dealt with your mother since the moment they turned me. Her plans...she plays a long game, Fortuna. Something about this feels too easy."

He wrapped his arms around me and kissed me.

Once I got my breath back, I pulled back and nodded. "Look, I know what you mean, but we're literally getting the entire gang together—"

"I don't like that I can't protect you during daylight," Chris said, cutting me off. His eyes were troubled. With a sigh, he brushed my cheek with his lips. "I won't lose you."

"Hey, I've made it this far."

Chris drew himself up slowly, and I felt him push away his concern. "That you have. Shall we?"

* * *

It took about forty-five minutes to go through the entire thing again. This time, Clutterbuck shared pictures projected onto Martin's clean white wall, passed around notes that his officers had written, and shared the audio of the meeting we'd tried to have with Prunella Noble.

My eyes widened. "You taped that?" Gideon, who I'd picked up earlier that afternoon, launched himself to his feet and growled at the chief. "Way to build trust, there, sir."

Clutterbuck stepped back. "Call off your hound, Delphi. The recording wasn't for evidence. I wasn't planning on sharing it with anybody at the station. It was for me."

"That violates about six regulations, sir," Gabe observed.

"How many does this meeting violate?" Clutterbuck snapped with a wrinkled brow.

"Daddy, how could you not tell her?" Angie said. She sounded disappointed. Angie's greyhound rubbed its head against her leg and whined while Gideon's growl took on an even more menacing timbre.

"Gideon, we've got this," I told the dog. Gideon bared his teeth in an angry grimace a final time and curled up at my feet once more. "See?" I told Chris in a low voice. "The dog's got me covered during the day. No problem." The greyhound lifted his head, stared at my vampire boyfriend, and sneezed on his perfectly creased pant leg.

Clutterbuck looked over the group reclining casually on various sections of a large sectional sofa. "I feel like none of you are taking this seriously," he said, his voice frustrated. "You're upset I recorded a conversation? About regulations? They shot a man in the head over this magical claptrap. A woman in my jail is being spotted at a church with one of my detectives. The three of you were strangers six months ago, and now suddenly you're all sisters—"

"Chief, take a deep breath and calm—" Gabe started, but his words stopped when Clutterbuck pointed a finger at him.

"Don't you dare tell me to calm down, young man," Clutterbuck said to Gabe as Martin rose from his place on the couch. The older man's voice was heavy and hard. "You have no idea how it feels to be responsible for the safety and security of a town that you don't understand! You are well aware they don't prepare you at the police academy for vampires and witches and magical holes in the ground—"

That got my attention.

"What did you say?"

Clutterbuck looked surprised at the sharpness in my tone. "What do you mean?"

"What magical hole in the ground?" I jumped off the couch and stepped up to Clutterbuck. Chris and Gideon moved into position on either side of me.

He blinked as if he wasn't sure what he'd just said. "What do you mean? You told me—"

"But I didn't," I cut him off emphatically. "I told you a lot, yes. I told you about almost everything. Almost." I turned to Martin. "I didn't tell him anything about your mother or any hole in the ground. I told him about the witch bottles, and the ghosts, and a bit about my mother." My face twisted like I was sucking on a sour lemon at the word. "But I never once mentioned anything about the hole in the ground. I promise I didn't. I'd never bring that up to someone I didn't fully trust."

"Someone must have," the chief said, looking pained. "How else would I know?" he murmured to himself. "There's no other way I could know that, is there? Angie?" Clutterbuck frowned as he searched around and met his daughter's eyes. "Angie, did you tell me?"

"No, Daddy." Angie set the papers she had been clutching on a side table and leaned forward. "Daddy, I've been trying to avoid talking to you about a lot of this magical stuff. It seemed hard for you to take, so I was just letting you get used to the fact that I was a witch." She smiled sadly at him. "I didn't tell you."

A fresh voice called out from the back of the room. "Do you think Karen is still controlling him?"

Aunt Addie stood in the archway between the living room and the kitchen. Her apron still on, a dishrag in her hand, she'd listened to the whole meeting without saying a word. Uncle Vito stood behind her.

They'd both silently listened.

Until now.

"I don't know," I told her. "I honestly don't know what my mother did to him that night." Thinking back to the night my mother came here to confront us, I tried to remember her exact words. "She said 'the chief is now mine again,'" I said with a grimace, giving voice to the image in my mind. "She said she wiped his memory of everything we told him about her, about magic belonging to anyone but her." I opened my eyes.

"But then you snipped the cords," Chris said. "So none of that would be true. Right?"

"Right, I snipped the cords," I agreed, but even I could hear the hesitancy in my own voice. "I snipped the cords from Karen to everything she controlled. Cords of connection, I guess you could call them. I snipped all the cords of connection." I was pacing back and forth, my arms crossed. I looked up. "That's not the only type of magic there is. I did nothing else. She cast a spell so he would forget," I said, waving my hand toward Chief Clutterbuck. "I cut all the cords, so if that spell needed a cord, he'd remember. And since he's remembered some things but not others, it's a spell that's still at work. It has to be. It's not like she cut those memories from his mind. They're still in there, buried by the magic that's slowly degrading thanks to the cord being cut."

"But that means..." Martin trailed off.

"Her magic is still in play," Pepper breathed as she grabbed Ollie's hand.

"The chief is still hers," Gabe said bluntly. "And they're in the same building all day. Who knows what magic she might cast?"

"No!" Angie told him fiercely.

"Do you have another explanation?" he asked her. "How would he know? Give me another explanation, Angie."

She didn't have one.

The room fell silent save for the whirring of the fan on the projector. Angie squirmed slightly on the sofa as she glanced at the others. Ollie looked shocked, Martin glum. Gabe put an arm around Dalida. Chris folded me into his arms. "It'll be okay."

"It's not okay. How did I miss this?" I murmured.

* * *

"It's not your fault," Chris told me as we stood on the terrace overlooking the town. "It's not your fault; you spotted it at the moment it was clear, and we're going to deal with it."

I shook my head. "The very fact he didn't remember her, that he arrested her at all. I should've seen it."

"You thought it was a consequence of you removing the cords."

I rolled my eyes. "You mean I got cocky and thought I was, like, super witch, and when I removed the cords, I would magically free him from her clutches. That's what you meant to say, wasn't it," I said sarcastically.

"If that's what I had meant to say, that's what I would have said," Chris responded evenly.

"Stop being nice to me. I don't deserve it."

The glass door slid open. "How's she doing?" Angie asked Chris.

"Am I such a screwup you can't even ask me directly?" I asked her without turning around.

"Oh, boy," Angie muttered.

"Leave me alone for a few minutes, Angie, huh? I just—"

"Oh, please," she shot back. "Fine, sis—you screwed up. You missed a magical thing that put my dad in jeopardy, and you screwed up. You should have known. You shouldn't have let this happen. We relied on you, and you screwed the pooch."

Angie's harsh words brought everyone out onto the porch. I whirled on her and glared.

"Gee, Angie, tell us how you really feel," Pepper laughed bluntly. "Don't you think you're a little harsh?"

"No, I don't." Angie turned to Pepper. "Fortuna's right. She messed up. Telling her she didn't will not change anything. We all got complacent. And she knew it, too." Angie glanced at me and raised her eyebrow. "You said it right here on that outdoor couch a few days ago. That we were all acting like everything was over. Like everything was wonderful."

"Even though there was one bottle left, and

even though Anna was still buried and held prisoner," I whispered.

"Exactly." Angie nodded. "You knew. We convinced you otherwise. And then you convinced yourself everything was fine. The last stretch. Time enough to deal with things later. And it's possible that our delay in finding the bottle just caused a man's death." Angie held up her hands. "Screwup any way you look at it."

"This is your idea of helping?" Pepper asked.

"We've all been a part of this for a while," Gabe said from behind her. "This wasn't just Fortuna. We all wanted it to be over. And we wanted the over part to be easy. The ghosts are all off hanging out—and sure, they're looking for the bottle, but not exclusively. We are all doing our own thing." He looked down. "Six months ago, none of us would have just gone out to eat or made vacation plans while two people were still imprisoned."

"Hawaii," Dalida whispered to Pepper's silent eyebrow raise.

"When this started, we were diligent. We've gotten less so, assuming the two people we had to rescue were at least safe."

"That was a legitimate assumption, though, Gabe," Ollie said.

"No, it wasn't." I shook my head. "I knew your father had something sketchy going on over at that church from way back. So did you. As soon as we knew that their beliefs had something to do with paranormals, we should have been digging into it. We didn't."

Ollie didn't want to agree, but finally, he nodded.

Dalida smiled. "So, no more dinners out, no more vacations. Not until we get this solved?"

"Oh, I don't know," Martin said with a half-smile. "Even in the middle of a crisis, we have to eat."

"And if you have to eat, it may as well be Beef Wellington?" Dalida teased me.

The group laughed.

I fought the urge to magically zap every one of them.

"So, how much longer are you going to sulk?" Angie cocked her head. "Because the problem you're out here complaining you missed?" She pointed toward the glass door. "It's sitting on a couch. I know my dad's done some bad things," my younger sister said, her voice growing serious. "But if he's just ensorcelled and we can fix it? We need to go do that. And yeah, maybe you made a mistake. Maybe we all should've caught it. But we caught it now." She paused for a few seconds, her eyes burning into mine. "And we need you to help fix it."

I wanted to sit and sulk more.

I was angry at myself for not paying more attention, for pushing my mother out of my mind so far that I missed she was still making moves and counter moves. That as much as I thought binding her not to harm anyone would end her reign of manipulation, I never made sure.

But my plucky younger sister was right.

It was time to end this once and for all.

TEN

"Before we get started with anything," I told Chief Clutterbuck as we all walked back into Martin's house like a mob on a mission, "where's the witch bottle you brought from the police station? We probably should have dealt with that before any of this."

"What witch bottle?" Angie's father stared at me with wide eyes. He looked almost drugged. "What's a witch bottle?" His head wobbled on his neck toward his daughter. "Honey, what is that woman talking about? Is she a friend of yours from school?"

My jaw dropped half a notch.

"The chief has been, um, decompensating since you all retired to the veranda to discuss the situation." Aunt Addie sat next to him on the sofa, her hand on his back. I wasn't sure if she was comforting him or keeping him from running away. Uncle Vito stood behind both as if he expected Chief Clutterbuck to jump up and become violent at any moment.

Though considering Uncle Vito was nearly eighty and Chief Clutterbuck was armed, I'm not sure what the old man expected to do about it if it happened. Regardless, he looked ready.

"What do you mean, decompensating?" I approached Clutterbuck, but his eyes widened like I was a tiger stalking my prey, and I stopped in my tracks. "Why didn't you get us?"

"He's fine, just...a little woozy, that's all. It seemed better to let him talk. He told me he has to leave, must return to the police station. That it's imperative. Then he tried to leave, but the two dogs"—Aunt Addie gestured toward Gideon and Ella—"convinced him it would be better if he waited until you all returned."

Gideon sent an image to me of a cuckoo clock clanging loudly.

Chris turned toward me. "Do you think she knows? Would it be possible at this distance?"

"That or we've tripped some sort of failsafe in the spell."

"My head hurts," Pepper said. She closed her

eyes. "Dalida's right. Hawaii sounds good right now."

"Let's not all start panicking here, okay?" I said with forced cheerfulness. "The only thing that's happened is Chief Clutterbuck got a little loopy, that's all. The house isn't shaking on its foundation. There's no lightning in the sky, no unexplained paranormal wind whipping the trees around. We're not under attack. The situation isn't any different from what it was five minutes ago when you were all outside telling me we could solve this with a little elbow grease and some creative thinking, then top it off with a Beef Wellington."

Pepper's eyes flew open, and she cast a dubious look at me. "Oh, for goodness' sake, Fortuna, are you trying to call up bad juju? Lightning, paranormal wind? Why would you even bring those things up?" Her eyes moved from me to the window. She stared out suspiciously. "Does anyone see anything?"

"Oh, calm down, Stanford. We mentioned that magic might be involved, too," Angie reminded me. "Do you even know what's wrong with my dad? Like, is it something you can sense with telepathy?"

"Not without diving into his head, no," I told her as I reluctantly stepped towards Clutterbuck. His eyes were unfocused, and he seemed agitated.

The closer I came, the worse it got. "Chief, do you know what you're doing here?"

"I'm here to protect my daughter," he answered in a neutral tone.

"I imagine that's exactly what you think you're doing, but I'm worried at the moment your answer can cut two ways," I told him with a sigh. "We are all concerned about you. You remember the presentation you just gave us about Karen? Conrad Noble's murder?"

That made him laugh outright. "I wouldn't have told you."

I pulled back and half-closed my eyes to make my vision hazy so I could examine the chief for silver cords. Something, I reminded myself with guilt, I probably should've done before this moment.

To be fair, no one had gone near my mother for months. And even if they had? I assumed my cutting the cord between her and Anna (Karen's presumed source of power) would negate any actual damage she could do from the bowels of the Mystic's End jail.

It never occurred to me she would have enough magical ability to re-forge those bonds.

And even if she had enough magical ability, I arrogantly assumed my binding her against harming anyone would prevent her from doing so.

As soon as I unfocused my eyes, I realized I'd missed the most obvious tie.

There, glowing clear as day, was a vibrant silvery-white cord hooked into Chief Clutterbuck.

Coming from Angie.

I sighed. I didn't even have to check. Still, I stood up and walked around the room to confirm another cord from Angie stretched taut in the police department's direction.

My sociopathic mother had used the blood connection between her and Angie to get her claws into Chief Clutterbuck once again.

The entire room watched me, silent, waiting to hear what I'd seen. I opened my mouth, then closed it. My eyes teared up unexpectedly. At that moment, I was so angry. Angry at my mother, for taking ties that were supposed to be comforting, something to be counted on, a place where people go to be safe and instead, turning those things against all of us.

Angie didn't deserve this.

None of us did.

Chris's voice finally broke the silence. I don't know how he knew, but he knew.

"I can tell you found a tie. I would suggest that we not bother figuring out how it happened. The most important thing is breaking that tie. Since it can be painful, I suggest that you and Dalida work the magic while Angie remains in the circle with her father."

"Why me?" Angie asked, confused.

"You're the healer." Chris smiled. "Or did you forget?"

She blinked in surprise, sighed, and then nodded. "I keep forgetting I can do that. Okay, Daddy, come on. You and I are going to lie on the floor." Angie stepped over to her father and reached down to help him up. He looked embarrassed at his unsteadiness, but he didn't protest. "Fortuna is going to fix your head for you. It won't take too long." My sister smiled at me. "She's gotten kinda good at it."

"I'll go get the candles," Aunt Addie said. "And if you need a third witch for the circle, my dear, I will stand with you. I may not be much of one, but you're family, dear." Before the older woman turned, she threw her arms around me. "You're a good girl. All three of you are. These burdens... they'll be gone from you soon." She pulled back. "But family, Fortuna? The family remains. That's the one thing my brother-in-law had right. Family's everything. And you? You are family."

I was dumbstruck at her spontaneous declaration, so much so I didn't know how to respond.

"Addie, why don't you go get the candles,"

Chris said, loosening his folded arms and stepping toward me. Once Addie scurried toward the back bedrooms, I stared at him, still speechless. "Breathe."

"I just didn't know what to say," I whispered. I glanced around the room, somewhat embarrassed, but everyone was moving furniture and clearing a space. No one had noticed, or if they did, they didn't stop to stare. "It was just..." I trailed off, unable to put what I was feeling into words. "What do you say to something like that?"

"You didn't have to say anything. That's the beauty of family, Fortuna. No one expects you to be anything other than what you are. Addie said what she said because she wanted to say it." The vampire half-smiled. "And because she meant it."

Still struck dumb by whatever was going on inside my head, I just nodded and turned to help Gabe push a chair across the room.

* * *

After we moved the furniture and the candles were lit, I wondered to myself why we'd bothered to do all that work. Sure, the first time I did this cord-cutting thing, we went full-witch in the library. Circle casting, candles, the whole nine yards. The second time I did it? I performed the entire thing from start to finish on a driveway while my mother ranted and raved. No one even knew it was happening.

Well, Chris did.

But Chris seemed to know everything.

I looked around the dimly lit room, the cleared space surrounded by concerned onlookers. Addie placed the candles at four points on the floor with measured steps and sober respect, as if she were moving to a drumbeat only she could hear. Admittedly, there was something beautiful about ritualizing the act, though. It felt more solemn than plucking cords from a raging madwoman on a driveway.

Gently laying Clutterbuck down, Angie beside him, I felt like I was playing the opening chords of a symphony. The gang surrounded us more closely, watching, and I could feel the energy of their concentration. Without being told, they arranged themselves around the circle, just outside. The room grew quiet, the power thick as Dalida, Addie, and I strolled around the edge of the makeshift area and leaned over to light the candles.

"We ask for the guardian's protection of those that enter this sacred circle," Addie intoned, raising her arms. Ollie glanced at her, kissed Pepper on the cheek, and stepped forward to light the fourth candle directly opposite Aunt Addie.

Uh oh. Um.

"We ask for the guardian's protection of those that witness this rite," Ollie called out. He fumbled in his pocket for a lighter and then leaned over to light the candle in front of him. I guess he still remembered that witch training from his college days. Even though he was completely human, it was touching that he wanted to help.

But, you know, no one said we were doing, like, a particular ritual.

"We ask for the guardian's strength to complete the work that must be done," Dalida said as she looked up, her face soft as her eyes blinked slowly. Breathing in, she leaned forward and lit the candle.

They came to me at the northernmost candle—not remembering what the heck I was supposed to say. Miss Bessie wasn't really a ritual type of teacher, and my lessons with Priestess Goodfellow were long past. My mind went blank. I'd never done a ritual that used the words everyone said, and it embarrassed me everyone seemed to know what to say—and I didn't.

Gideon shoved an image in my mind. Me, painting. And painting again. And painting again.

His message was clear—just say what I felt.

So I did.

I closed my eyes and breathed deeply. "May all the guardians protect those of us within the circle, outside of the circle, and gift us with the power to set the wrongs of Mystic's End right." I opened my eyes, looked down, and was shocked to find my candle glowing brightly even though I hadn't lit it. A bubble of white-silver shimmered around us.

"Whoah," Pepper whispered.

I met Chris's gaze through the iridescent bubble as I turned. He nodded once.

"What now?" Angie asked nervously.

"Just lie next to your dad and keep skin to skin contact with him so this doesn't hurt." Ollie and I nodded to one another, and he took up a position at the pair's feet.

"What do you want me to do?" Dalida asked nervously. "I don't have any special powers like you and Angie. I'm just a run-of-the-mill person who can talk to ghosts." My fraternal twin shrugged and looked down sheepishly.

My jaw dropped. I didn't know whether it was the magic of the circle, the heavy energy of the night, or what. I suddenly realized that my sister Dalida had a unique magical power. And it was the exact opposite of mine.

"Of course you do. You projected the ghosts."

"Oh, yeah, really useful," she told me quietly.

"I don't think you projected the ghosts, though, Dalida. I think you project. Period."

Dalida looked confused. "What do you mean?"

"I'm a powerful telepath. But you? I think you are, too, just the other way. You didn't project the ghosts. You projected the ability to see them into everyone's mind that couldn't. I mean, that's...that's huge." I sat back on my heels. "I can pull things out of people's heads, but sister dear, I think you can put things into them."

Her eyes opened wide. "That's...that's terrible. You can't be right."

"No, it's not terrible, and I—"

"Would you two get on with it?" Angie seethed, popping up to a sitting position, pointing at her drooling father.

"While I'm cutting the cords," I said to Dalida, ignoring Angie, "you try it."

"Try what?"

"You want her to just test out a power she doesn't even think she has on my dad?" Angie said between clenched teeth. "Fortuna, are you out of your—"

"You can do it." I looked at Angie. "She can do it."

Dalida shook her head. "But what if I—"

"Just project into the chief's mind. Project into his mind that he is safe, he's whole and can access all of his memories. Project that he, and only he, is in control of himself."

That brought Dalida up short. Her eyes narrowed. "That's it?"

I nodded. "That's it. Force of will can overcome an awful lot—"

Just then, Clutterbuck tensed and seemed to spasm as if having a seizure. Ollie jumped up toward his midsection and stared down at the man's red face. Grabbing the chief's wrist, his eyes went wide after a few seconds. "You need to hurry," he told me. "I don't know what this is, but his pulse is racing—"

"Damn! Sorry, sorry!" Angie flung herself back down and wrapped her arms around her father. His muscles relaxed, and the spasm slowed. After a few more seconds, it stopped altogether. "Guys, he doesn't look so good. I know I'm supposedly some super healing touch person, but this is making me nervous." Her father's face had taken on a dusky hue. "You said I can only make people feel better. I can't make them better." She gave me a pointed look. "Make him better."

"Okay, let's do this. Everybody ready?" Dalida and Ollie nodded at me. Angie clutched her father tighter. "You know what you're going to do?" I asked my twin. She stared back at me, nervous, but then nodded. "Okay. Here we go."

* * *

For all the drama surrounding the ritual, it wasn't really much. It didn't take long for me to unhook Karen's tie from Angie. Once that happened, Clutterbuck's face lost its ashy gray pallor and returned to normal. I was thankful I could solve the issue without damaging the bond between father and daughter. That was a cord I wouldn't have been comfortable cutting.

"It was strange," Dalida told Gabe and me afterward. "I was so nervous about doing it, but it was like I simply walked into his mind, stood in the center, and told him how to feel."

"Uh-huh," Gabe nodded, his voice slightly shaky. "That's great, dear. I think it's wonderful." The detective looked a little pale.

I raised an eyebrow. "Do you?"

"You must be thirsty. Let me get you both something to drink." Gabe Wilcox bolted toward Martin's kitchen like we had shot him out of a cannon. I guess it is somewhat alarming realizing your girlfriend can just shove whatever idea into your head she wants you to have. I bet Gabe would do a lot of dishes if they ever married.

A lot of dishes.

"Anyway, it seems to have worked," I told Dalida. "I poked around in there, and he seems much healthier than he was an hour ago." The three of us turned to watch Clutterbuck, who was lying motionless on the couch, snoring. His body appeared to shut down after the ritual and worked on finishing the healing we'd begun. "I guess we'll know more when he wakes up."

"It's just bizarre to me it was that easy."

"What?" I asked Dalida. "Manipulating someone's mind?"

She nodded.

"I was quite surprised the first time I did it," Chris said as he walked up and joined us. "It seems like people should have more defense against manipulation than they do, but it's not something that comes naturally to them. Their urge is to trust, to believe, to be open to new people and new experiences. That, and I think there are so few paranormals with these abilities, over time they have to think any defense against psychic manipulation is unnecessary."

"Psychic self-defense is the first thing we learned when training as human witches," Ollie said as he and Pepper walked up. "I guess that's why humans still study witchcraft and still practice it in places. Some people remember."

I nodded. "How's Angie doing?" I asked Pepper. She'd just left her side.

"I don't think she'll be okay until he wakes up, but she came through the ritual just fine."

"That's good."

"So, do we have to worry about all the officers at the Mystic's End Police Department being under Karen's spell now?" Gabe asked. "We didn't see her control of Clutterbuck coming, and if it was because he was in the same building with her or was around her—"

"We don't," Chris said with finality.

I nodded. "I agree with Chris. The reason Karen could get her hooks into him again was for..." I turned and looked at Angie, wanting to explain to the group what happened but not wanting my sister to know that our mother came through her.

"It was a reason other than proximity," Chris said. "And if there's anything I've learned about Karen White, she doesn't waste her time or energy controlling people that aren't powerful."

Gabe looked back and forth between us and then shrugged. "At least it's resolved now."

Well, something was resolved.

We still didn't know who killed Conrad Noble, where the witch bottle was, who stole the selenite sphere and why, and what was going on at the Holy Grove Church. Other than that...

Yeah, actually, we'd resolved almost nothing.

ELEVEN

Chris watched the dozing chief of police like an owl staring at a moonlit lake. "I think he's waking up."

The slack-jawed, drooling Clutterbuck stirred slightly, took a deep breath, and slowly opened his eyes. Ollie laid his fingertips on the chief's thick neck and nodded as if he was happy with what he found there. "Don't get up too fast," the assistant coroner warned him. "I'm not entirely sure what you've just been through, but your body decided you needed a break from everything to get over it. You should probably listen to it."

"Do you remember anything?" Angie asked her father.

He smiled weakly at her. "I remember you

protecting me." Clutterbuck reached out for his daughter, and she helped pull him to a sitting position. "That's not right, you know. Fathers protect daughters, not the other way around."

"You raised a tough chick, Daddy," my younger sister told her father with proud satisfaction. "We protect each other."

The chief frowned. "I didn't protect your mother." His face twisted into shock and then horror. His enormous hands flew to his face. "Your mother's death was my fault. This has all been my fault. Everything from beginning to end."

"I don't think that's the case, sir," Gabe replied crisply.

"You don't know the entire story. None of you do." Clutterbuck seemed to fall again, his head lolling as if he was about to doze off. Then, with a start, his eyes opened again, and he looked more alert than he had been. "Karen didn't just threaten Angie. Didn't just kill my wife...if she did? Like I said, there was no evidence." He winced as if the memory was physically painful. "She claimed to have captured my wife after her death. It wasn't bad enough that Tara's car ran off the road. It wasn't enough. Karen insisted she could torture my wife for all eternity if I didn't do what she wanted."

Chris and I looked at one another. "The last bottle?" he mouthed silently.

"I ran for Sheriff when I was younger, did you know that? Won, too. I quit because Karen wanted me to be chief of police instead. So Martin could come here and..." The chief blinked his bleary eyes. "I told you this. I'm sure I told you this. But I couldn't have. Wait, did I?" For a moment, he looked confused. There was a long, almost fearful pause. "I told you about Tara, didn't I? About my wife, and the car accident." Suddenly, he looked at his daughter with a terrified expression. "You know about the affair. Oh, God, honey, I am so sorry—"

"Daddy, you've been through a lot, and it's clear that Karen was messing with your head. I know everything, and I'm not angry. She's a terrible person. It wasn't your fault. You're only human." She reached over and grabbed her father's hand, pulling it to her and enclosing it with her other hand. "Right now, though, we need you to tell us what you know. You and I will have plenty of time to talk about the past now that you remember."

"You didn't kill your first husband, did you?" Chief Clutterbuck suddenly asked, his eyes narrowing.

"You couldn't have left some things hidden, huh, sis?" Angie said to Dalida in a defensive tone.

"Sorry." Dalida shrugged. "When you've got it, you got it," she added with particular pride.

* * *

Angie and her father continued talking. Chris was a master at being patient, but as they continued discussing their family history and forgiveness, I watched his patience slowly run down like a weak battery on a phone. After ten minutes, he sighed loudly—even though he didn't technically need to breathe air. As the conversation turned to yet another topic that promised to be long-winded, the vampire stepped toward the pair.

"Chief, I'm sorry to interrupt, but we really need that bottle. Did you bring the witch bottle from evidence?" Chris asked in a neutral tone. Martin stood behind his vampire bodyguard, trusting him to direct the situation where it needed to go. Their interplay was interesting—as if they passed a leadership baton back and forth depending on the situation.

For a few seconds, I wondered who, exactly, was ultimately in charge of whom.

"The bottle, the one in Conrad Noble's hand," Chief Clutterbuck said as if just remembering its existence. "I didn't bring it here, no. I went into the evidence room to get it, and I saw it on the shelf, but then I...I don't really know what happened. I just turned around and walked away without it. I was sure, in my mind, it wouldn't be needed."

Martin and Chris glanced at one another and nodded, but I overheard no telepathic words pass between them. "Can you check the chief before we decide on our next steps?" Chris asked me. "I want to make sure that there's absolutely no one else in his mind other than him." Martin smiled and nodded.

"Sure," I nodded. I reached out, lifted Clutterbuck's chin, and gazed deep into his clear eyes. Sensing thoughts, sensing feelings, going through memories...I'd been doing it so often that the inventory took little time. "There's no one in there but him," I told Chris, standing back up straight.

"The way I see it, we have three things we need to concentrate on," Martin said, stepping forward. "One is the witch bottle. Chris and Fortuna can accompany Chief Clutterbuck to the police station so we can get it. The two of them are the strongest in the group—"

"Hey, I have a gun," Gabe objected. "Fortuna still pales around firearms. And I used to work there, so I know the place, and I know the people."

"Forgive me, I didn't mean to insult anyone's prowess," Martin told the detective. His voice held a hint of amusement. "Chris and Fortuna are the most adept magical users in the group—"

"I can make anyone happy just by touching

them with the teeny tiny tip of my finger," Angie protested, crossing her arms. "If someone stops us and is suspicious or questions us about what we're doing, don't you think that would come in handy?"

"Like I said," Martin repeated slowly, sounding a little more impatient. "We have three things we need to concentrate on. One is getting the witch bottle, so Chris and Fortuna can accompany Chief Clutterbuck to do that. The second thing we need to do is find out what's going on at the Holy Grove Church." Martin turned toward Ollie. "Are you comfortable bringing Pepper over to the church to do a little reconnaissance? I know Reverend Kane is your father, and so I wouldn't ask you—"

"I'm fine," Ollie replied confidently. "It will not be a problem."

Pepper rummaged through her bag. "I can wire us up so we can get audio of everything."

"I really do like you, but sometimes you scare me more than Fortuna," Angie mumbled.

Pepper beamed.

"And the third thing?" Uncle Vito asked raspingly.

"The third thing we need to figure out is where this land is and why it's so important that someone would shoot Conrad Noble to get it in the hands of the church," Martin said finally. "Since an attorney that used to work for the complex signed the papers,

I think Angie and I would be the best people to handle that."

"What about Dalida and I?" Gabe asked. He sounded a little sullen if you want to know the truth.

"You guys go round up the ghosts," I said, cutting off whatever Martin would say. Chris looked at me, quizzically. "We know where the last bottle is so they can stop looking for it. We need some of them to go monitor Karen in jail and tell us if she's performing any magic or if anybody looks like they're under her spell."

"And the rest?" Dalida asked.

"Have them look for Conrad Noble's ghost."

The entire group looked slightly taken aback.

"I thought the ghosts in Mystic's End disappeared somewhere?" Gabe asked, confused. "Isn't that part of the whole weirdness of the town? That there should be ghosts, but there aren't?"

"And yet there's a border at the edge of town keeping the freed witches from getting out of here," I told Gabe. "The more ghosts we've had checking out that barrier, the more suspicious I've become that the ghosts in town couldn't leave even if they wanted to."

"I agree with Fortuna that something is off. Spike and Plum have been working diligently on trying to get through the barrier, finding a break in it, finding a hole in it," Dalida explained in her soft voice to Gabe. Turning to the rest of the group, she tilted her head. "They have found no such weak spot. It seems unlikely anything incorporeal could go through it anywhere."

"Can't they just get through the barrier with magic?" Pepper asked. "Like, maybe there is some kind of phantasm ejection spell?"

"Ejection spell?" Ollie asked, trying to cover a laugh.

"Well, I don't know what to call it! I don't know the limits of this stuff."

"It's a legitimate question, but I don't think so. I haven't been able to get the ghosts we know out, even with magic. Like I said, it's just a hunch, but I think they're still here. Somewhere. I hoped—well, I hope—when we open the last bottle that they'll be..." I struggled to find the right words. "Look, like I said—it's just a feeling based on what we've learned."

I had dealt with these magical bubble barriers before. The Magical Midway had been in one of them. I knew from my friend Charlotte that specific people could be allowed in, also allowing particular people out. She told me, though, if you were dealing with many, many people crossing the barrier each day—like, say, a town—it was much easier to allow and disallow people by type. Based on that, I believed it likely no ghosts could leave Mystic's End.

Also based on that, the fact that there were no ghosts other than the freed witches…

Well, there was Miss Bessie. She and I had talked about it, and she believed the mystic power had protected her from whatever curse might be at work on the dead. Joe, a dead mailman, also lived in the town as a specter, but he'd gotten caught in a quartz crystal when he died. That seemed to have prevented him from disappearing to wherever everyone seemed to go.

"Gabe, I agree with Fortuna. I think it's worth looking into, and I also think that none of us should wander off doing these things alone," Martin admitted. "They already shot someone in the head this week. We need to make sure we stay together in pairs and that at least one person is armed." He looked pointedly at Ollie. "Do you have a gun?"

Before Ollie could pull out his weapon, Pepper yanked out her own substantial black handgun.

"You definitely scare me more than Fortuna," Angie told the reporter, her eyes wide.

"Yeah, but I have my charm, right?" Pepper chirped as she stuffed the pistol back into her knapsack.

* * *

"I think she's been casting spells on me," Clutterbuck huffed from the backseat as Chris drove a huge Cadillac Escalade toward the police station. "Whenever I came to talk to her in her cell, I put my hands on the bars. She'd always reach out her hand, you know? I thought nothing of it because we used to be involved. I thought she was just trying to get me on her side."

"You thought nothing of it because she didn't want you to think anything of it," I responded, glancing back at the chief in the rear-view mirror. "Telepaths are very tricky magical users," I admitted. "Considering all three of her daughters have some type of telepathic ability—"

"I thought Angie was a healer?" Clutterbuck asked.

"She is, but she makes people think they're happy, feel bliss. Her first husband was suffering from cancer and in a lot of pain. When she touched him, that pain went away—the cancer didn't. She couldn't heal the actual disease, but she could make it, so his brain didn't interpret the pain that his nervous system was telling him was there. Telepaths mess with people's brains in different ways, so really, Angie's just a specialized telepath."

"Well put," Chris said.

"This is all so strange," Clutterbuck mumbled.

"I'm happy to have my memories back, though, so thank you. I feel totally in control of myself." Just before we reached the main road, we spotted a patrol car parked. Clutterbuck waved happily through the window, not realizing the tint wouldn't allow his cheerful wave to be seen. "I feel really safe. Secure. I mean, you've got this, right?"

"If your sister could bottle that, she'd make a fortune in the pharmaceutical industry." Chris glanced in the rear-view mirror, raised his eyebrow, and shook his head. "Chief Clutterbuck, sir, you may be feeling a little overconfident. Residual effects from the ritual, sir."

"Oh, yeah?" I could practically hear Clutterbuck's smirk. "This is better than a massage out at the complex. I should have one of these once a week. I feel great. Hey!"

"Sir?"

"You're not really a vampire, are you?"

"Yes. I really am, sir." Chris's tone was polite.

"I didn't think there were any vampires. You don't drink blood, do you? That's a myth, right?"

"No, sir, that's not a myth. Vampires drink blood."

There was a long pause. "Not going to drink my blood, are you?" Clutterbuck asked apprehensively.

"No, sir."

"Good, good, good," the chief answered nervously.

Chris glanced at me and smiled. I smiled back.

A few minutes later, the silence was broken again.

"So, ah, not even if you get really thirsty?"

TWELVE

When the three of us entered the police station, the officers on duty greeted Chief Clutterbuck with friendly nods and pats on the back. "Evening, ladies and gentlemen," he called out jovially. "How's the evening going so far? Everything pretty calm? Calls about average for the middle of the week?"

"Yes, sir. It's been a good night, sir," the young, fresh-faced Officer Corbin answered from behind the reception desk. "Officer Locke took a complaint from the Mayor about her neighbor's dog barking, but other than that, it's been pretty quiet." He glared at me as if it was my fault the mayor had complained about her neighbor's dog. "Most of the guys are out on patrol. Detectives left a few hours ago." The young man glared at me once more and then moved his eyes toward Chris. "Oh, Mr. Jeeves, sir. I didn't see you there." Officer Corbin stood up straight and nodded. "Good evening to you. Can I get you something? Coffee? Tea, maybe?"

"Evening, Blake. Nothing for me, thank you."

Blake? First name basis with the police?

Of course.

"Boy, Martin's money really buys you the red carpet reception, huh?" I mumbled, annoyed at Blake's apparent preference for my companions. The officer's self-important smirk after overhearing my comment grated on me even further.

"It does, in fact," Chris responded with a chuckle. "I've never understood why someone having money changes the behavior of those that don't have it or makes those that don't have it more respectful of people that do. My lack of understanding doesn't change the fact that I have realized it's more often the case than not."

"That you get a red carpet?"

"Indeed."

Officer Corbin struggled between a smile and a frown as he listened. I could tell he thought he should be insulted by what Chris said, but he wasn't sure why. Glancing between the three of us, he noted my annoyance. "I'm sorry, were you thirsty?" He asked more out of obligation than concern, as if just realizing he'd been ignoring me.

"Officer Corbin, when I was in here before, you mentioned that your mother wasn't fond of me. Or, more specifically, that her church wasn't fond of me. Is that right?"

"I'm sure I don't know what you're talking about." Officer Corbin grabbed his mug and turned, covering the six feet between him and the coffee machine in record time. "Are you sure you don't want a cup of coffee? I just made a fresh pot about a half-hour ago."

"I'm sure," I called across the space. Clutterbuck opened his mouth to say something, but I reached out and touched his arm. "I'm just curious because it seemed like your church was really interested in getting me to come worship there. At least originally. It doesn't seem like—if you thought I was evil—your Reverend would be interested in that."

The officer turned, holding his mug in one hand and the coffee pot in another. "Reverend Kane wanted you to worship with us?"

"He sure did." I nodded. "So, I'm kinda confused why you seem to be...I don't know, unnerved by me somehow." I kept my tone level, conversational even. The officer tilted his head like a confused puppy.

"Well, for a while, we thought you stole the sacred orb. It turns out we had misplaced it, and you didn't. But while we were looking for it?" He made an angry face and paused long enough to pour his coffee. "We had a lot of not so very nice things to say about you and your kind. But like I said, it turns out we were wrong."

"How sacred could the orb be if you misplaced it?" I asked wryly.

"Pretty sacred, ma'am," he responded. "It looks just like the one you have in your shop. That's why we thought you took it. But, like I said, it just got misplaced. See, everyone in the men's group takes a turn caring for it. A few of us are a little more responsible than others, and one guy—Saul—accidentally left it in his toolbox." Officer Corbin took a sip of the coffee and looked up. "Or was it Seth that left it in the toolbox?"

"It's not important. Why is it sacred?" Officer Corbin looked back down at me. He seemed confused why someone like me would want to know about the orb.

"The mystic orb? Well, gosh, ma'am, it holds the history of the town."

"An orb?" Chief Clutterbuck, Chris, and I glanced at each other. "How can an orb hold the history of the town? Is it some kind of electronic device? Like a computer or weirdly shaped tablet?"

"No, ma'am, it's not electronic at all. Like I said, it looks just like the one in your shop."

"The one in my—"

"The crystal ball," Chris whispered so low that only I could hear him. "The one on your front table."

My mind flashed to Reverend Dexter Kane's reaction the first time he spotted the crystal ball. He nearly turned white, even though it was nothing more than a run-of-the-mill spherical selenite ball. I'd like to claim there was something special about it, but there wasn't. I bought it because it looked like a moon, and it was pretty. I charged it with protection spells, and that was that—just a crystal ball.

"Just one more question, Officer," I said. "Was Conrad Noble in your men's group?"

"Well, sure he was." Corbin's face fell as he remembered the recently deceased accountant. "He and his wife Prunella come to church all the time, ma'am, and she insisted he join the men's group. Duty, you know." Officer Corbin looked around as if checking to see who else could overhear the conversation. Then he walked back to the counter and leaned forward, glancing at his boss. "I don't think Brother Noble really enjoyed the men's group, though. Actually, I don't think he really enjoyed church at all, if you want to know the truth. At least not lately."

"Why would you say that, Officer?" Clutterbuck asked.

"I know I'm not supposed to listen to people when they talk, but last Sunday?" Clutterbuck, Chris, and I leaned forward. "I heard Bond and Conrad fighting. They were just outside the auditorium doors. I couldn't hear what they were saying, but they were furious. Well, angrier than they usually are. Like I said, I don't think Conrad Noble enjoyed church too much." Corbin's face fell. "His brother seemed to always waylay him after services, and they always got into an argument about something."

"So it wasn't the church that Conrad had a problem with?" Chris asked.

"No, Mr. Jeeves, I don't think so. But the fighting got a lot worse a month ago, and I heard Prunella talking with Reverend Kane about how she thought Conrad was going to quit. She asked him—the Reverend—to talk him out of it."

"Quit church?" I asked.

"I think so. I guess it doesn't matter now that he's dead, but it seemed like they were having problems."

Just then, an older woman stormed into the station. "I want to report my neighbor! Who do I talk to? They keep parking their stupid truck three feet over into my property line, and I want somebody to get them for trespassing if they do it again!"

"Ma'am, I can help you right over here," Officer Corbin called out with a wave. "I sure hope you find out who killed Mr. Noble. He was such a nice man. He was always kind to me. He didn't deserve what happened to him."

* * *

"I'm sure everybody's thinking the same thing," I said as soon as the elevator doors closed.

"Well, of course you're sure. You're a telepath." Chief Clutterbuck chuckled and poked me, his face bright.

"You're in an excellent mood considering everything we're dealing with," I told him, arms crossed.

"I told you, I feel great, totally in control. I am utterly confident that we will solve this case, and then we're going to go out and get some of that Beef Wellington Martin promised. I'm really looking forward to that dinner. I've never had that. Too expensive," Clutterbuck confided with a wink. "I know everybody thinks I'm just rolling in money because of all the bribes and things like that, but I'm really not. Mostly, Karen just threatened me." He nodded as if that settled it.

I wasn't sure precisely what Dalida had done to him—although I was the person who directed her to do it—but whatever she'd done had turned Clutterbuck into a walking, talking advertisement for the positivity that comes from overconfidence. It was like dealing with an older, male version of Pepper.

"I thought your daughter was a millionaire?" Chris inquired politely.

Clutterbuck stared at him, his expression horrified. "I would never take a dime from that girl. Not a penny. It's not for parents to take from their children; it's for parents to provide for their children. You don't have children, do you?"

"No, sir."

"No, of course you don't. Vampire, I almost forgot. My apologies."

"For what?"

"Well, vampires can't have children, can they?"

Chris glanced at me for a second and then returned his eyes to Clutterbuck. "Vampires can have children, yes."

Chief Clutterbuck stopped his smiling, jovial look then. He turned and studied Chris's face, his eyes drifting to the vampire's mouth. His face paled.

"I don't mean any disrespect, son, but that's damn horrifying."

Just when I thought it might be the longest elevator ride in the history of elevator rights, the indicator dinged. The door opened—to the dingiest, darkest, dimmest hallway I'd been in since walking through the haunted house at the Magical Midway.

"Shall we?" Clutterbuck asked as he stepped out.

Chris and I followed.

* * *

Describing it to Pepper later, I likened it to the beginning of the labyrinth in David Bowie's epic '80s movie. I looked right, and I look left. Both directions seem to go on forever.

"Is a really tiny worm with a shock of blue hair going to come out and offer me a cup of tea?" I asked, drawing closer to Chris.

"I love that movie," he murmured as he reached for my hand and squeezed.

"Didn't I mention that the evidence room is in the old lower level?" Clutterbuck asked.

"I thought this entire complex was new? Martin donated money to build it, and you guys moved from the center of town to here, right?" I asked.

The air felt humid and oppressive. Even though

it was evening, the police station above—new, clean, and modern—had been bustling with a fair amount of activity. Down here, the corridor was empty. So empty I could hear our voices echo out into the darkness. A darkness that seemed to press in.

"Well, that's true, mostly," the chief nodded. "But they built the station on the old Lambert place."

"What's the old Lambert place?"

"It was an old plantation. It was falling down, but the basement where they kept the workers—"

"The slaves," I corrected.

Chief Clutterbuck rolled his eyes at me. "The workers—"

"The slaves," I corrected again.

"For heavens' sake, they kept people down here," Clutterbuck said with an air of frustration. "All right?"

It felt like we were miles below the surface, deep underground. I'd heard what Clutterbuck said about who stayed here and its purpose, but I wasn't sure I believed that. Like everywhere else in Mystic's End, I saw no spirits, no ghosts. The hallway seemed energetically hollow and empty.

But...not.

Whatever this was, it wasn't a bunkhouse for slaves. I was sure of it.

"Could this have been a mine?" I asked him.

"I told you what it was."

"No, you told me what you were told it was," I responded. Somewhat to my surprise, Clutterbuck thought about it and glanced around. "I'm just asking, because if it's a mine—I mean, how far do these hallways go, anyway?"

"Are you thinking this is how someone is getting Karen to the church?" Chris asked.

"Well, almost exactly in that direction,"—I pointed the dark passageway leading toward the complex—"is Martin's stuff, right? And directly next to that in-between here and there is where Anna is. If we go that way?" I pointed the other direction. "Wouldn't this beeline straight toward the church?"

"It would have to go all the way through town," Clutterbuck said as he stared into the darkness. "The church is on the other side of town from the complex."

"Not really." Chris shook his head as Clutterbuck turned to face him. "The complex is directly across from the prison. The church is in between the two, a little off toward the edge of town. If you were going to measure distance as the crow flies, I doubt it would be more than a couple of miles."

"That's still a really long underground walkway to dig," I told him.

"Not if a bunch of witches carved it out by magic," Chris countered, raising an eyebrow. "Or, not even looking at magic, what if you're right and this is an old mine? Some mines can go on for miles. There are coalfields in Arkansas. In the river valley."

"That's not that far from here," Clutterbuck said. "Anyway, the evidence room is right down here. Let's get what we came down here for. Because between you, me, and the bricks? This place gives me the creeps a little, too."

I raised my eyebrow. "I didn't say it was creepy."

"You didn't have to."

We walked for another thirty seconds until we came to a heavy wooden door.

A wooden door.

A heavy wooden door?

Why would an evidence room be behind a heavy wooden door?

It wasn't just any door, either. The top of the door was a proper arch. A perfect one hundred and eighty-degree radius fitted into the corresponding frame. Its thick, dark wood looked like it had been recently stained and sealed. This entryway seemed more appropriate to an old-world church or castle than a police station evidence room.

A sizable electronic scan pad was affixed to the

stone to the right (looking entirely out of place). Sheriff Clutterbuck took out what I presumed was an ID and scanned it. The light at the top of the pad went from red to green. The door clicked.

Clutterbuck pushed it open, turned, and gestured for us to come in.

I took one step toward the room and slammed back into Chris as the air and energy whooshed into me. We both went flying into the opposite wall and landed in a heap on the floor. (Well, I should clarify. I landed in a heap. On top of Chris. Who had somehow managed—while we were flying through the air—to wrap his arms and legs around me so he would cushion the impact.)

"Are you all right?" he asked me, his eyes concerned.

"Why wouldn't I be all right? I basically just bounced off you," I told him, brushing myself off. We both stood up and looked at Clutterbuck, who was gawking back out at us with his jaw open wide. "So, they warded your evidence room against witches? Or telepaths. Or maybe just me."

Chris attempted to walk across the threshold and flew across the hallway—although where I had tumbled rear end over keister, Chris flew through the air like an elegant cat and landed on his feet. "I think it's warded against paranormals. I could try to speed in there, but if the force with which it throws me has an exponential relation to the force I exert on it, I could hurt myself."

"Neither of you can come in here?" Clutterbuck asked, incredulous.

"Nope. That's fine, though. Just grab the witch bottle, and we'll go. You're right," I told him. "This place does kinda give me the creeps. And I don't really creep easy."

The longer we were in the hallway, the more I felt like I was being watched. Chris seemed slightly more alert than he usually was, which was also never a good sign. "Do you hear anything?" I asked the vampire with the super hearing.

"No, I don't. But that's not the odd thing," the vampire said, lowering his voice. "I feel like I should. I sense there is something near to hear, and yet I hear nothing."

He put his arm around me, and we waited silently for Clutterbuck to return from the magically warded evidence room.

I wished that time had buried this place long ago. Maybe slaves had lived here in the darkness, perhaps this was a way to traffic people, possibly it was a mine. I didn't know, but the longer I was down there, the less I wanted to know. That someone had magically warded the evidence room?

That was just icing on the creepy cake.

"You're not gonna believe this," Clutterbuck said as he appeared at the door.

"The witch bottle is gone," Chris guessed.

"Still holding onto that confidence that we're going to solve this, Chief?" I asked him.

Chief Clutterbuck didn't answer.

THIRTEEN

"So, what do we do now?" Clutterbuck asked me.

"Give me a minute to think." I leaned against the opposite wall and stared at the warded door.

It seemed like I was losing track of things, and I needed a minute to center myself. Just to reevaluate what we were doing. On the whole, I would've preferred to center myself lying on a couch with my dog and a cup of tea, but I was learning we can't all have exactly what we want in Mystic's End.

"How many levels below the ground are we?" I asked Clutterbuck.

"This is level B6, so six or seven."

"There is no level B. The basement is B1. So, six levels," Chris added, watching me.

"If the height of each story is roughly 15 feet," I mused, eying the ceiling, "we are roughly 90 feet below ground. Give or take." I thought back to my climb down the hidden hole. "That seems to be more or less even with Anna's tomb-ish thing. At least as far as I can guess from memory. I can't believe that's a coincidence."

Clutterbuck nodded. "That's the place only you can get into, right?"

"Not only that, but only paranormals can see it," Chris reminded him.

"Have you ever gone down that way, Chief?" I pointed right toward the darkness. "Where does it stop?"

"From what I understand, they bricked up both ends to keep anybody from getting lost down here. There's just storage, and it's all pretty close to the elevator here."

"Storage? Besides the evidence room, what else is down here?"

Clutterbuck shrugged. "Police storage, evidence storage. Unused furniture, old uniforms. You know, just stuff."

"But why here? Why six stories below the surface? Is there something wrong with levels B1 through B5?"

"We're using them."

"That seems an excessive depth to build down to," Chris murmured, gazing in the complex's direction. "If there is an end to this hallway, Chief Clutterbuck, I don't sense it."

Clutterbuck looked Chris up and down. "Oh, right, you have that sonar stuff. Like a bat."

I could tell my boyfriend was trying not to chuckle at the lawman's use of Bram Stoker's Dracula to inform himself about Sparkles' superpowers. Finally, he shrugged. "Sure. My bat powers. I can sense several doors down in that direction, but there's no wall. Suppose I wanted to go in that direction. In that case, I could do so at a relatively quick speed without being concerned I would hit anything soon. If there is a wall, it is definitely beyond the bounds of this property."

"Should we go look?" Clutterbuck asked. His tone made it clear he wanted to do anything, absolutely anything, other than to look.

"No, just wait a second. There's got to be a way to pull down these wards," I said, glaring at the door. "Maybe the bottle is in there. Maybe someone hid it with magic. Stand back," I warned both men. "I'm a witch, darn it. I can get these down."

* * *

"I have no idea how to take these down. No idea. None," I told Chris and Clutterbuck an hour later. A thin sheen of sweat covered my body, and I was panting. I was furious, and I fought the single-minded determination demanding I stay there all night lobbing lightning bolts if I had to. "What am I even doing here? If these are on the church, too? I may as well just go home and cuddle up with my dog. I'm useless."

"You are not," Chris told me sternly. I looked into his deep brown eyes. They shone with so much love and warmth my tiny tantrum embarrassed me. "You have no idea what they put into that spell. It's quite possible they were made more complex just for you. Just so you couldn't take them down."

"Is Karen that good at planning?" I asked as I pulled my shirt away from my body and back again rapidly to facilitate air movement.

"I told you once not to underestimate her."

I stared down the darkened endless hall and tried to calm myself. I felt like I was running around in circles. Each lap I took piled another weird thing right on top of the last bizarre thing. It was a teetering tower of weirdness.

An accountant having a witch bottle and a crystal ball. An accountant being shot in the head.

The church needing a piece of land so much that someone may have gunned down the accountant to get it. Two places I went to—about this murder—being warded against me. Me!

And to top it all off, I contemplated all this in an honest to goodness dungeon with a corridor so long and so dark I couldn't see to the end.

With the chief of police and my vampire boyfriend.

Weird upon strange upon bizarre. Why was this even here? Who put this at the bottom of a jail? My patience for all this intrigue was wearing thinner than my oldest pair of sweatpants. I was growing weary of the twists and turns.

"How far into the future could she have been planning?" I said, more to myself than anyone else. "Could Karen have known there was a chance they would arrest her, and have planned or facilitated this? Because this makes little sense otherwise. Constructing a brand-new facility that's modern and state-of-the-art, but leaving the dungeon intact? Why would anyone do that?"

"What's more, building an elevator down to that dungeon. That room is not the most obvious choice to keep evidence in. Chief, you never answered me before," Chris reminded Clutterbuck. He repeated his question regarding the five floors above our head and what they were used for.

"Cells. B1 is the visiting level, processing. That includes a couple of twenty-four-hour courts to get the misbehaving tourists in and out quickly. B2 and B3 are the men's cells. B4 houses women. B5 are the high-security cells, and isolation cells, and the medical facilities."

I cursed loudly in surprise that a literal Alcatraz was sitting on my head. Clutterbuck winced.

"Look, the complex may have their own security force that can pass people off to us, but they can't house people. We have 336 cells in the whole place, though we rarely get close to that. Thanks to Martin's taxes and donations, we don't have any reason to run it at capacity. I think we are about on par with the prison on the edge of town."

"The number of cells for a small town jail seems wildly excessive."

"Remember, we share the jail with the county. Some smaller neighboring towns house people here as well," Clutterbuck reminded me, shifting slightly. He seemed to get a little defensive.

As well he should.

"I just never thought a town with a few thousand residents would have something like that."

The chief turned and closed the door, locking it. "We're not your average town, Fortuna."

"Oh, I'm well aware of that, Chief Clutterbuck. Your evidence room just blew me across a dungeon corridor to make sure I don't overlook that insignificant fact."

"I still don't understand that." Clutterbuck walked away from the archway and turned to stare at the wooden door. "We've had no reports of anything like that. I've seen nothing like it until today."

"Why can't I put this all together?" I asked Chris. "This just seems like a jumble of weird things that don't go together."

Chris looked at me oddly. "It seems related to me, Fortuna. Clearly so. That Conrad Noble's home was warded to keep you out, and this evidence room was warded the same way? That's far more than two weird things that don't go together," he said, surprised. "We know that your mother has magical ability left because of what she did to Chief Clutterbuck. We know she was seen at the church when she should have been a few floors up in a jail cell. The witch bottle is missing. The sacred orb, also missing." He tilted his head. "I feel you may be trying to pull these things apart because you know if they are all related? They lead back to one place. And it's the one place you don't want to go."

I took a deep breath. "You think I'm being deliberately obtuse."

"I didn't say that."

"Because if I stopped being deliberately obtuse, it would be clear to me I need to go speak to my mother."

"I would never call you obtuse," Chris said thoughtfully.

I waited. "So you think I should go talk to her?"

He continued watching me.

After waiting another twenty seconds, I snapped, "You don't have any observations beyond that?"

"I don't think I need to give voice to them. I can see in your eyes you know what the answer is."

I hated that he was always right. And I hated the way he always sounded super smug but totally caring all simultaneously. It made it very difficult to hold on to my indignation.

"Fine, but...I want a few more answers before we go." I pointed down the darkened hall that seemed to lead directly to Anna and Martin's complex. "I want to know where this goes."

"Now?" Clutterbuck asked, startled.

"Now," I told him.

And I began walking.

* * *

As we slipped into the darkness, I lit an orb of light to guide the way. The further we got from the elevator, the darker and dirtier and dingier the hallway became. Initially, everything was empty and quiet. As we crossed into areas utterly unoccupied by storage units, I could feel the eyes of tiny animals glaring at us as we passed.

"I thought you said there was a door blocking the path?" Chris asked the chief.

"I was told there was."

"You never checked?"

Clutterbuck made a sound. "Would you come down here if you didn't have to? Maybe it's further down."

"It's not," Chris assured him. "I'm sure. There's no brick wall."

"Sparkles can see in the dark," I told Clutterbuck as we walked confidently forward. "The whole place isn't lit up for him, but he can see three or four times as far as we can."

"Well, maybe we should just send him down there to check everything out, then."

"You know, you have a gun."

"I can't shoot what I can't see. Your little magic light ball is pretty, but it's not exactly bright."

"I don't think you need to shoot anything," Chris told him. "There's nothing here." He stopped walking. "I know you said that I should check everything out in jest, but it might not be a bad idea.

If this walkway really is several miles long, do we really have the time to do this?"

"There's no clock ticking on figuring this out," I shrugged.

"Unless you count my bedtime." I rolled my eyes at the reminder that my boyfriend had an allergy to the sun. "Or that we know of. Just in case there is, though—I can move far faster than the three of us can together. Or," Chris said, raising an eyebrow, "I could bring you both with me."

"There's no water down here. I don't want to vomit."

"Why would you vomit?" Clutterbuck asked me.

"Sparkles here can move really fast. I've mapped it out twice, and it's well over two hundred miles per hour. We are really not designed to fly through the air bouncing around like that. It makes me a little nauseous."

"Cars go faster than that," Clutterbuck scoffed.

"Not with me in them," I answered dryly.

"What do you think?" Chris glanced at both of us. "Should I go on my own and report back?"

"I'm just concerned there's going to be something only I can see. What if there's something like Anna's hole, and you blow right by it because you can't see it?"

"That's possible, but even if there are things I

can't see? I'll be able to tell us where this goes, if anywhere. That's more information than we have right now, and I can get it in much less time."

"How much less time?" Clutterbuck asked him.

"If it's two miles, I can be back here within ten minutes." Chris met my eyes, a hopeful look on his face. "Faster if I take a few risks and push my speed."

I frowned. "You will take absolutely no risks, and you'll be back here in fifteen minutes. Because you will be extra careful."

The vampire looked disappointed, but he nodded and promised me he would. "You'll take care of her?" Chris asked the chief of police politely.

"While we are standing here doing nothing?" Clutterbuck responded with a chuckle. "Sure. No problem."

Chris took a slow step forward. It brought him face to face with Clutterbuck, their noses almost touching. "You'll take care of her?" the vampire asked again—three times as slowly. His eyes narrowed, and his fangs extended. Somehow looking even paler than usual in the glowing supernatural light, his entire body seemed to vibrate with tension.

It was the first time I'd ever seen him look

genuinely frightening, and my breath caught in my chest.

If I was struck by Chris's sudden change, though?

The chief looked like he was about to pee in his pants.

"Absolutely," the nervously earnest Clutterbuck responded. "As if she were my own daughter. You have my word."

Chris stood there for another five seconds, his silence absorbing the oath. With a nod, he stepped back, retracted his fangs, and relaxed the tension in his muscles.

"You didn't have to scare him," I chided the vampire.

"And as for you, Fortuna, stay here," he said, turning. "Even if you suddenly get a bright idea. Even if you just want to check that thing out that you heard or saw or thought of. Unless something comes to the spot and attacks you and you have to run," Chris lectured, his fingers dancing lightly on my chin. "Please, please, just stay here."

"I'm not Pepper," I grumbled and then kissed him. "Be careful."

With a whoosh, he disappeared.

After a few moments, I heard the chief's quiet voice. "Doesn't that hurt?"

"Doesn't what hurt?" I asked, leaning against the wall to wait.

"The fangs. When you kiss him. Doesn't that hurt?"

"Kind of none of your business. But no. Kissing Chris is like kissing anyone else."

As soon as the words were out of my mouth, I realized I didn't know that for a fact. I didn't know what it was like to kiss anyone else. I'd had minimal experience with dating and almost none with relationships. Intimate partnerships with people when you're a telepath? They're not a straightforward thing. I found no one I cared enough about to try.

Until Chris.

"You doing okay?" Clutterbuck asked.

"Surprisingly, yeah." And I meant it. I had an exceptional dog. I had two sisters. I had a great circle of friends. And my boyfriend could bite anyone that made me mad. Actually, my dog could, too.

I was super close to freeing the last witch stuck in a bottle—and Martin's mom. I mean, I wasn't Charles Lutz or Harriet Tubman or anything, but it felt good. Being close to accomplishing something that once seemed so impossible.

Suddenly, I frowned.

What did Officer Corbin mean? The history of

the entire town in their "sacred orb"? That had to be symbolic, right? But if it was just symbolic, why would someone steal it?

What did that ridiculous church have to do with all this?

And why was it so important Conrad Noble had to die?

With another whoosh, Chris reappeared. "You were right. This path goes all the way to Martin's complex. Or, more specifically, Angie's restaurant."

"The underground hallway to get to the club?" I asked.

He nodded. "The door to the right, about midway through the tunnel?" Chris asked me. I nodded. "There's a set of stairs that goes down six flights. There are three doors at the bottom, and one leads to this hallway."

"So the construction of this precinct and Martin's complex both accommodated this path. But why?"

"Probably for easy access to the cauldron," Chris said. "Big one, about halfway to the complex. It's in an open antechamber. Very obvious, you can't miss it."

"Why would you need a tunnel for access to a big pot?" Clutterbuck asked, confused.

"It's not just a big pot," I explained. "Witch cauldrons are ensorcelled communication and teleportation devices. Most people just have small ones to use to call other witches—"

"Why not just use the telephone?" The chief still looked confused.

"Because of the teleportation aspects," Chris explained. "You can talk to someone who is very far away, but as long as they have a cauldron, you can reach through the mist and pass items. If it's a large enough cauldron on both ends, people can also simply step through."

I nodded. "I take it this one's big enough?"

"If we wanted to throw a hot tub party and invite ten of our closest friends? I think we'd be good."

The three of us started back toward the police precinct. We were silent, each contemplating what on earth Karen White had been planning for Mystic's End that involved this level of preparation. Giant cauldrons, underground quick access tunnels to the police station and the track, controlled armies of paranormals, unlimited funds, bribed and blackmailed town leaders...

Three daughters, placed with rich or influential families.

What did my mother, ultimately, want?

A new fear gnawed at me.

A fear there was too much of her well-planned blueprint left in play for this to be over.

FOURTEEN

When the elevator door opened, Clutterbuck stepped inside with one long stride. Chris and I followed, turned, and waited. The chief reached out and hit the button marked B4.

The women's jailhouse floor.

"No." I shook my head. "I'm not ready to talk to her."

"Ready or not, she's like the center of a hurricane you're circling around. You can only measure the wind speed of a storm in the eye, Fortuna," Clutterbuck responded. He then hit the button to close the doors—which, let's be honest, does nothing. I mean, I'm sure they do nothing. I don't know why anyone bothers to hit the things.

The doors seem to close when the doors decide to close. "We all know that whatever's going on here? It leads back to her."

"We just think that. We don't know that for sure." Granted, if someone else was at the center of all this, darned if I knew who was. "We really should get with the others first and find out what they might know. Maybe someone got a critical piece of information we need. Maybe it will point to something we haven't even thought about yet." Clutterbuck raised his eyebrow. "What? It's just not necessarily her."

Clutterbuck glanced over at Chris. "I thought she was a psychic?"

When Chris met the lawman's gaze, there was just a hint of menacing. "Respectfully, for a man that just recently had no awareness of things he'd done or the control Karen subjected him to, you're rather insensitive about this. I'd suggest you cut Fortuna some slack as she works her way through this situation."

Clutterbuck harrumphed, mumbled under his breath about being plenty sensitive, and redirected his gaze at the door.

"Don't you think I should go get my sisters?" I whispered to Chris, hoping I could delay the inevitable. "If I'm going to talk to her, maybe they should be there."

He responded with a look that contained sympathy—and the knowledge I was grasping for excuses to delay the inevitable. "I'll go in with you. It's probably a better idea that I accompany you, in any case. I've had a much longer relationship with Karen than you have, and I'm much better acquainted with her than either of your sisters." His eyes tightened with concern. "Besides, according to your visit from Beulah Conroe, your mother is demanding to see you. Not your sisters."

"I'd almost forgotten about that." Add another weird brick to the pile.

The elevator doors opened, and we came face to face with Detective Beau Conroe, Beulah Conroe's son. "Where are you three going?" I noted that Conroe showed no surprise at seeing the three of us there.

Our suspicions about Detective Conroe came rushing back. The words I'd heard in his mind about the same thing happening to Clutterbuck was another weird brick on a pile that was towering. Chris sensed my sudden tension and moved closer, his alert eyes scanning the blond Conroe for any visible threats.

Which there was because Conroe was carrying a gun.

"I'm taking Fortuna to visit her mother," Clutterbuck said, walking forward in such a way as to present Detective Conroe with the choice of slamming into the big man or giving way so his superior could pass. For a moment, I wasn't sure which he would choose. Just when I thought the two men would physically collide, Conroe stepped back.

"It's not visiting hours." I could sense the detective's glee I was here—even as he worked to hide it.

"Well, it's a good thing I run the whole place, then, isn't it?" Clutterbuck said, motioning for us to follow him down the hall. Before we could follow, Clutterbuck halted, turning on his heel to face the detective once again. "By the way, Detective Conroe, I went down to the evidence room to look at Fortuna's bottle. I wasn't able to find it. Since Noble's murder case is technically assigned to you, I figure you must know where it is." The chief cocked his head. "Where is it?"

Conroe's mind was blank as he stared back at his boss. "I'm sure I don't know. I haven't been down there. Probably just got filed in the wrong place. Why would anyone steal some old bottle?"

"I didn't say anyone stole it, Detective. I asked if you knew where it was."

Detective Conroe shot a look at me—as if getting caught tipping his hand was my fault.

"My mistake. You all have a delightful visit

now." Conroe jabbed the button for the elevator far more aggressively than he needed to, and the doors popped open. Stepping in, he glanced back. "I'm sure Ms. White will be happy to see you." Before any of us could answer, the doors closed.

"What a turd that guy is," Clutterbuck mumbled.

"He's going down." I pointed to the arrow on top of the elevator. "He's not going back up to the main station; he's going down." I turned to look at Clutterbuck. "Why would he go down? There are only two floors below this one. The high-security floor, and the dungeon."

"It's not a dungeon."

"It looks like a dungeon," Chris disagreed. "Could you have missed the bottle? How hard did you look?"

The chief gazed up at the ceiling and whispered to himself, running through all the places he checked. We waited for Clutterbuck to get through his thorough step-by-step mental inventory. Finally, he shook his head. "No, I looked everywhere that thing could be. I mean, I didn't pull down all the boxes and rummage through them, so I guess I can't swear that the bottle wasn't anywhere in the room. But I don't see how it would get in a box in the first place."

"What do we do?" Chris asked me.

"We need to follow him," I said as I hit the button as aggressively as Detective Conroe had. "Do you think he's in the evidence room, or is he walking toward the cauldron? Should we just gloves-off this thing?"

Clutterbuck looked at me. "Gloves off? What does that mean?"

The elevator doors opened and I stepped in. "We need to stop all this sneaking around. We are not getting anywhere, we have none of the things we're looking for, and no one else is exactly tiptoeing around us. Beulah Conroe came to see me and demanded I see my mother. I've tried to walk into places today that blew me with a gale-force wind in the opposite direction." I held up my hands. "We're the only ones being subtle. Sneaking around, looking, poking. We're getting nowhere."

"Are you saying you want to stop being subtle?" Chris said, stepping into the elevator. Clutterbuck stood in the hall, looking concerned. "Because I can stop being subtle."

"Hey, I work here, and not everyone in this place is corrupt, you know," the chief told me nervously as he walked into the elevator and hit the button to head back down to the dungeon. "Let's not start drinking people's blood and throwing sparkly lightning bolts at people in the middle of the station. I will not be able to explain that."

"You can throw sparkly lightning bolts?" Chris whispered as Clutterbuck glared.

"I don't know." I shrugged. "Maybe we should find out."

* * *

The corridor was quiet. If I didn't have a vampire with me, we might not have known which direction Detective Conroe had gone. But I had a vampire with me, and Chris immediately scented him.

"He's gone toward the cauldron room."

Clutterbuck raised his eyebrow. "That way? Are you sure? He's not in the evidence room?"

Faster than the human eye could see, Chris shot down to the evidence door and then boomeranged back within seconds. "No. His scent isn't strong on the door at all. I can tell that he's been there before, but not recently."

"What's recent to you?" the chief asked.

"Maybe in the last six hours. If I had to guess, the last time he was in that room was around three this afternoon."

"Your nose is that precise?"

Chris nodded once.

"That's just creepy," Clutterbuck muttered.

"But useful," I chimed in. "Can you tell with

that super sniffer of yours whether he had the bottle with him?"

Chris shook his head. "I don't know what the bottle smells like. If it had been in your possession, there's a good chance I could tell. But since you've never laid hands on it?" He scratched his neck, his head tilting. "I can't isolate the hints of it. It may be there, but I wouldn't know it."

"So do we follow him?" Clutterbuck asked.

"I don't see why we all need to follow him. I am a vampire." Clutterbuck held up his hands in mock surrender and then rolled his eyes. "It was simply an offer, Chief. I am more than capable of going to get him. I can deposit him back here within seconds."

"But he's got a gun, hun." I knew they involved Detective Conroe in this. Still, I didn't know if he was interested enough to kill on behalf of whatever conspiracy he was helping to further. I didn't want to take any chances. "You could get hurt."

Chris's posture stiffened. Looking down at me, he gave me a half-smile. "I would be incredibly offended at what you just said if you weren't so adorable. Incredibly offended." The half-smile turned into a broader, playful grin. "I promise you, my love, the gun the detective is carrying will be of absolutely no consequence. None. In fact, he'll be quite surprised how little it—"

"Okay, no, that's the creepy thing. Yep. That right there." Clutterbuck crossed his arms and took what seemed to be an unconscious step back. "I think I liked it better when you both pretended you were human."

"Okay, go," I told him. "But don't hurt him. Just—"

Before I could finish the sentence, a breeze wafted across my face and a whoosh hit my ears.

I don't want to say that my nice, very caring vampire boyfriend seemed overeager, excited even, by the prospect of dragging the detective back here by his short hairs. I don't. I really don't.

But if someone asked me if my nice, very caring vampire boyfriend seemed overeager and excited by the prospect of dragging the detective back here by his short hairs, I would probably remain silent.

It's hard to explain to someone that your predatory partner is actually a nice guy.

Better to just not mention some of those inconvenient dichotomies of nature.

Clutterbuck and I waited.

Within seconds, we heard a thump from the darkness. Then a scream. Then another thump. Then, out of nowhere, Chris appeared clutching the detective by the shirt front. When the vampire released his hold, Detective Conroe tumbled to the ground as if his legs were no longer particularly useful.

He was disarmed; his face was smudged with dirt, but he wasn't bleeding, and there were no teeth marks anywhere on him.

"Do you often go for an evening walk down a dark tunnel under the station, Detective?" I asked him.

Conroe stared at Chris, his shoulders curling as if he expected a blow. "What are you?" he asked the vampire, his voice shaking. "What the hell are you? You're not human, are you? Oh, God, I think I'm going to have a heart attack."

"I assure you, you're not," Chris told him.

"Where were you going?" I asked.

"What did you do to me?" Conroe was so shocked at the sudden violence he couldn't take his eyes off Chris's hands. He wasn't paying attention to any of my questions. "What are you? Answer me!"

"Son, do you really think you're able to demand answers? I mean, you're on your knees on the ground. I see your sidearm is gone. You don't have the upper hand here." Clutterbuck's voice was calm, almost soothing, as he spoke to the frightened man. "Surely you've seen more alarming things in your time working for Karen, haven't you?"

"How do you know I was working for that

woman? Who told you?" His voice was high-pitched, almost hysterical.

"Well, you just did, son." Clutterbuck did his best not to let the guffaw be too condescending.

But it was pretty condescending.

"You know nothing that's going on!" he spat. Conroe's attempt at showing fight and fire failed as the spittle dripped down his chin. It only made him look more frightened. "You people and your stupid political games. There's something bigger here, Chief, and you're on the wrong side of it! You have no idea!"

"There is a reason I flew down the hallway to grab you, Detective—and clearly, finding out more about what's going on would be one of the top reasons. If not the top reason."

"Where is the witch bottle?" I asked in my third attempt to get Detective Conroe's attention. I didn't know if it was because I was the least threatening person out of the three of us, if it was because the guy was a misogynistic jerk, or if I just wasn't speaking clearly enough to get my question across. But for whatever reason, Conroe was ignoring my questions as if I wasn't even asking them.

Which was, admittedly, annoying me.

"What's a witch bottle?" he asked, his eyes confused.

"The bottle that Conrad Noble was holding

when he was killed. The one you signed in to evidence. The one that's now missing. Where is it?"

"I don't know anything about it," he said, his voice lowering.

"You are lying," I told him, as sure of his lie as I was that the sun would come up tomorrow.

"You don't know that!"

"Actually, she does, son. Don't you remember Fortuna's a telepath?" Clutterbuck reminded him.

"She's a devil woman," he whispered fearfully.

Chris struck Detective Conroe with his open palm. It was a light tap, really, on the back of his skull—with just enough pressure to get his attention. It was so light that in other circumstances, I'd have considered it a friendly whack between friends. But because it came from Chris?

The detective screeched like his underwear was on fire.

"Okay, okay! I gave it to my mom! My mom said the church needed it!"

In unison, the three of us glanced at one another over the white-faced, shaking, half-crying Conroe.

"Why would the church need a bottle?"

"It belongs to the church—"

"The hell it does," I snapped, tensing. Chris

reached out and laid his hand on my shoulder. "That bottle does not belong to your church."

Conroe stopped blubbering and looked at me. "My church? I don't go to church."

I blinked. "You are not a member of the Holy Grove Church?" I asked, surprised.

"No. I guess it might be easy to think that. I occasionally go there with my mother. But no, I don't pay dues or have any membership or go to any of their secret meetings. That's my mother's thing." He swallowed nervously. "But I believe in what they're doing. I don't know that I believe everything they say, but...but I believe enough."

Chris and I glanced at one another. "What is it they think they're doing?"

Conroe pursed his lips as if he wasn't sure whether he should answer. Then with a nod, he did. "Protecting the town, of course. That's why it's so important you talk to your mother. If they don't do their prayers, and that church folds? Well." Conroe looked at Chris and then me. "I mean, look at the two of you. The town's already in trouble, isn't it? You're here. Everything Reverend Kane preaches about. Everything the church tries to prevent. You two are kinda evidence of that. Your being here is a sign that the church is failing, that the town is in trouble."

We're a sign that—

Suddenly, in the blink of an eye, it all clicked.

I had expected the reasons behind the church's existence to be more secretive—something dark, something sinister, and something well hidden. But between what Detective Conroe was saying and what he was thinking? Going back through the things his mother had said? Learning the town history from the ghosts?

Suddenly, it all snapped into place.

I could see the church's role in Conroe's mind. His mother believed the congregation to be the only bulwark against paranormals devastating the town again. Returning to reclaim what they'd lost so many years ago, invading for vengeance. Poltergeists, pixies, zombies, witches, vampires... The Conroes believed without the church, without Karen, they would return.

Their town history wasn't buried. The victors rewrote it as a tale of threat against the men that destroyed the Delphi coven. The humans that had triumphed over the paranormals that founded Mystic came up with stories to ensure the townspeople remained vigilant. That history developed and morphed and now lived on in that church—Mystic's history given new life and a new purpose.

The Delphi coven came here to protect itself against humans and fell.

Now, these humans believed they were protecting the entire town against the return of the paranormals and the fall of what they built. The cornerstone of their beliefs was the fear we would do what their ancestors did to our ancestors.

And yet...they fell. They just didn't know it.

The church wasn't secretive about what it believed—not really. The whole rigmarole about blood devils and devil women and...It was right in front of my face the entire time. Their paranoia, their fear repeatedly proved by the curse that killed the descendants, was a historic fear reinforced by those strange events.

And then one sociopathic witch was born.

My mother put it all together to exploit their karmic dread to the fullest—for her own gain and no matter who got hurt.

A whispered tall tale passed through the generations made real—for power.

FIFTEEN

I wanted to ask her why she did what she did. Was she born this selfish, this power-hungry? Or was it something that developed in her over time? I wanted to look into my mother's eyes as she answered. I'd be able to tell if she was lying.

Suddenly, that urge to hear the truth from her own mouth was almost painful.

"What do you want to do now?" Chris asked as Detective Conroe eyed me fearfully.

I was ready to go talk to my mother.

But I couldn't bring myself to say it.

So, maybe I wasn't so ready.

"Did you kill Conrad Noble?" I asked Conroe directly.

His eyes widened in surprise. "Me?"

"Oh, don't act all wide-eyed and innocent." I crossed my arms while staring down at him. "You just got finished telling me that your church thinks that saving the world—"

"Not the world. Not my church. They think they are helping the town—"

"—by doing whatever it is you guys are doing. You also said that ball—"

"I told you, I'm not a member of the church—"

"But you agree with what they're doing, and you have a gun—"

"Well, yeah, I agree with what they think they're doing, but I'm an officer of the law! I wouldn't break the law, and I certainly wouldn't murder somebody!" Whatever else Beau Conroe was hiding, the statement was genuine.

He was shocked—shocked, I tell you—that I could think he was a murderer. It surprised me it hadn't occurred to him he looked guilty of something.

"What about that argument between Conrad Noble and his brother at the church?" Chief Clutterbuck asked.

"What argument? What are you talking about, chief?" There was confusion in his eyes.

"Just how much investigating have you been doing, Detective?"

"Well, boss, you kept getting in my way!"

Conroe answered hotly. He jerked upward, and his muscles tensed.

"Settle down, there, Detective," Chris murmured. "Restrain yourself from making any moves I might...misinterpret."

Conroe glanced over his shoulder at Chris and sank back down to the floor.

"Have you been helping my mother leave her cell to visit the church?" I glanced down the hallway the vampire had sped through to retrieve him. "You haven't told us what you were doing down here, and you obviously know about this underground corridor and where it leads. You know more than you're letting on."

"Well, obviously. But that doesn't make me a murderer." He rolled his eyes to the side and flinched as he caught Chris's deepening stare. "Look, I know what you are. You're the bad guys. I don't know what you told the chief or why he's down here helping you. But you are the problem. Karen told us that someday you people would return to destroy the town, and you're obviously—"

"Wait, slow down there. Why do you think we're the bad guys?" Clutterbuck asked him. "I mean, exactly. Be specific."

"Because you are hanging out with the witches and vampires," Conroe said like it was obvious. "You used to work with Karen, boss! You know they are the bad people! I don't know what happened to you—or who got to you—that you turned on Karen and everything she's done for this town—"

"Karen may have been responsible for my wife dying, Detective Conroe," Clutterbuck barked at the younger man. "So, whatever you say next, whatever you think you need to say to me? Keep that in your mind before you utter your next words. I've been having one hell of a week, and my patience for people's crap is wearing very, very thin."

"I don't think she was."

All three men turned to stare at me.

"You don't think she was what?" Clutterbuck asked.

"I don't know that my mother actually killed anyone," I admitted. I explained Miss Bessie's description of the curse—that women who challenged the town leaders would mysteriously die. I told them how many ghosts I'd been able to recover and how many women had been captured more than a hundred years ago. "From everything we've learned recently, it seems that the curse causing deaths isn't on the entire town. I think the curse is active on the descendants of the Delphi coven, and it might only be activated when they anger descendants of the men that founded the town."

"That's why people aren't just falling over dead every time a man and a woman get into a fight," Clutterbuck said.

"Right." I nodded. "But Karen's ancestor—the witch that started the curse—could have made it with any parameters. The deaths were infrequent, but they sped up over the past twenty years or so." I looked, took a deep breath, and gazed back up. "Maybe my mother uncovered exactly how this curse worked, and she used it to her advantage."

Before I could say any more, Clutterbuck turned white. "My family...Our history..."

I turned to him with as much sympathy as I could muster. "You are the descendant of a town founder, aren't you?" He swallowed and nodded. "It's possible that's why she targeted you. Also possible she knew how to manipulate you both so that the curse—"

"Don't say any more. Just don't say any more." The chief looked slightly queasy.

"Look, all I'm saying is that my mother never seems to get her hands dirty." I turned to Chris. "She created an army of paranormals she could control. Did she ever step in herself? Or did she always send all of you off to do her bidding?"

Chris shifted uncomfortably. "If you had to ask me point blank for something she'd done? Specifically?" He tilted his head and looked lost in thought. "Even Dalida's explosion...She got someone else to do it." The vampire frowned. "She seems very careful to keep her hands clean."

"She's only in jail because Martin turned on her," Detective Conroe pointed out. "We all know it. His money and power protected her before."

"Hope no one's got a recording device on them," Detective Conroe said under his breath.

Clutterbuck glowered. "When he turned on her, her protection was gone. Karen used to—"

"More specifically, Martin's father," Chris corrected.

"Yet again, keeping her hands clean. Pulling strings that appeared to be held by someone else," I added.

Detective Conroe looked up at us, his face troubled. He pushed himself up unsteadily and turned. "You're making her sound like some kind of criminal mastermind."

"If the shoe fits." I shrugged.

"You have to be wrong."

"Well, there's a simple way to find out, isn't there?" I held out my hand to the detective. "Come upstairs with us to talk to her. See if what she says to us is what she's said to you or what you know from your mother. You used to be Gabe's partner. He said you're a good cop." I half-smiled. "Mostly."

He paused as if considering, then nodded. "Okay."

"If you see anything hinky, if you find a reason not to trust her, you'll tell me where the witch bottle is?"

Detective Conroe paused again and stared at me. Then he nodded a second time.

* * *

As far as jails go, it was nice.

"Why, Beau, you didn't have to accompany my daughter to visit me," my mother said in a singsong voice. She was lounging, relaxed, on a thin mattress in her cell. Wearing pink pajamas shining brightly against white silk covered pillows, my mother didn't pull her eyes away from the television. She could have been home watching Netflix and chilling instead of locked up awaiting trial. "Have you all seen this show?"

I glanced at the television and recognized it instantly. It was the latest documentary about a serial murderer. Not the type of fare I would've watched if I was behind bars. "We have some questions for you," I started, but she held up her hand.

"The show will be over in just four minutes. Surely you can let me finish—"

With a wiggle of my finger, I sliced the power cord in half. The screen went dark, and the back of the television smoked.

"Maybe I shouldn't have placed you with the Addingtons," my mother said flatly. "Clearly, they didn't teach you any manners."

"They taught me plenty of manners. I know which fork to use and everything," I responded in an even tone. "Why did you send Beau Conroe's mother to get me here? What could you possibly have to say to me at this point?"

Karen White slowly lifted the silk sheet covering her legs and moved them delicately to the floor—where her matching fuzzy slippers waited. Once her feet slipped in them, she reached for a matching robe.

She took an extraordinarily long time to put it on—as if she were putting on a show and had to establish the pacing.

"Is that any way to speak to your mother?" Karen asked as she tied it closed. Glancing to my right, she raised an eyebrow. "You, vampire, have been far more trouble than you were worth." Throwing her head back imperiously, she stepped toward Chris. "How is your sister doing? Still well, I presume?" Her tone dripped with menace.

Chris hadn't been a vampire long. Martin's father extended an offer to him when he was alive.

Become a vampire (and Martin's bodyguard) in exchange for a pile of cash and the magic that could permanently heal his ill younger sister.

The cash was from Martin Senior.

The magic was Karen's.

We believed that my magical binding of Karen —a spell preventing her from harming anyone— protected his sister. So far, we had been right.

So far.

It didn't mean she would not get her sociopathic jollies reminding him of the risk she posed.

"If you threaten one person in this place, I'm out of here," I told her angrily. So angrily, we attracted a guard's attention down the hall. I paused while Clutterbuck assured her everything was fine. Once her head pulled back with a nod, I turned again toward my mother. "What do you want from me? You better spit it out, because I don't want to be here one second longer than I have to be."

"The image of me you've built up in your head, Fortuna, is so much worse than the reality." My mother turned her attention to the posse surrounding me. "Why did you bring all these men with you? Send them away, so the two of us can talk. Mother to daughter."

Chris's neck and shoulder muscles tensed. Even though there were metal bars between my mother and us, he was warier of her than I'd ever seen him of anyone.

He probably wasn't wrong. I could sense danger, but I couldn't have put a name to it if anyone asked me to. Didn't know what direction it was coming from or what (if anything) I needed to be on guard for. It felt like we had walked into a trap. As if I should anticipate an attack I couldn't see and probably wouldn't avoid.

Suddenly, Miss Bessie's head popped out of the wall.

"You're fine," the ghost told me. "Mary and I are here watching. If you want to send the boys away, you can. We're here with you. We can run and get Chris if needed."

"Have you been here the whole time?" I asked, unable to cover a laugh.

"Where else would I be? I'm in jail, Fortuna," my mother answered sharply.

Miss Bessie nodded behind her. "Dalida and Gabriel told us you needed someone to watch her."

Mary's head popped out. "That woman has the most gruesome taste in television shows. Just vile. Not surprising for her, considering. But still. Just vile." The ghost shuddered. "Give me *Downton Abbey* any day."

"Did you overhear anything?" I asked Mary and Miss Bessie.

"What are you talking about?" Karen asked, looking frustrated.

"Plenty," the ghost answered as my mother stared at me strangely. "She still can't see us. I still do not know why."

That was clear. Karen growing more and more agitated by my ongoing conversation with her back cell wall.

"I even flew at her and tried to whack her about the head a little," Mary added. "She is entirely blind to the dead. Deaf, too. I had a bit of fun screaming at her."

"That was fun for you, was it?" Miss Bessie said, rolling her eyes. "It's a good thing I don't have a head, I supposed. I would have been down with a stellar migraine."

"You don't have ears, either. Or a mouth. Didn't stop you from complaining that I was too loud."

"You were too loud," Miss Bessie snapped back at her daughter. Mary simply rolled her eyes.

"Do you want us to go?" Chris asked me.

"Wasn't the whole point to bring Beau up here so he could listen to what was going on?" Clutterbuck asked the vampire.

"I won't be alone," I told them without elaborating. I stared at Chief Clutterbuck. "Give my mother and me a few minutes of privacy. Let me see what she has to say. I promise Chris will know the second things aren't going okay, and you guys can rush back in. The guard room is just ten feet away."

"The guard room," Clutterbuck said, raising his eyebrow. He glanced back out toward the more comfortable waiting area, and then once at the small guard room. "You want us to wait in the guard room?"

We'd walked in through the employees' hallway —a corridor my mother, as a prisoner, would have been unlikely to see. Since she would also be an unlikely visitor to a church while incarcerated (and yet was seen there?) I had to consider she might know there was a bank of surveillance equipment in the next room.

But if she didn't, she'd have no idea the three men would wait in a room with audio and visual surveillance centered right on us. They would hear and see everything—and know that my demand for privacy was a bogus one.

"Yeah, you guys should wait there. That should be fine, right?" I turned to my mother and deliberately allowed her to veto the idea.

"Just close the door, so we can have privacy," she told Chief Clutterbuck. "I don't want anyone to overhear."

The chief nodded and agreed as he shuffled Chris and Detective Conroe into the next room.

The heavy metal door between the two spaces clanged shut and then locked.

My mother stared silently at me, drifting across her cell at a contemplative pace.

"How could you get into a relationship with the vampire?" my mother asked me.

"That's where you want to start this? Trying to play mommy and making comments about my romantic choices?" Vampires had incredible hearing. Even without the audio-visual help, Chris could hear everything happening in this room. My mother had to know that—since she had an army of vampires just a few months ago. What was she playing at?

She stopped mid-stride and turned toward me. "I don't have to play mommy, Fortuna. I gave birth to you."

"You gifted me like a set of china plates to a rich family. Hoping you could come back and claim the wealth you adopted me into," I told her while swallowing the resentment I had over my youth. "You adopted me, a part-witch, to a woman who hated me because of my telepathy." I scowled, remembering the fury of my adoptive mother and my confusion as a young child. "Come to think of it, my adoptive mother would have been right at home at the Holy Grove Church."

"Your adoptive parents wanted you specifically

because of your powers," Karen told me. "So, I find your story hard to believe. You were supposed to help them become even more rich, even more powerful. They valued you like any good asset."

The bile in my stomach churned.

"You find my story hard to believe? You have a lot of nerve accusing me of lying. A lot of nerve." I said, incredulous. She didn't answer, but I digested the look on her face while resisting the overwhelming urge to punch it. "You know what? This doesn't matter. None of this matters. I left my family over ten years ago. I made my way in the world without them and without their money. I haven't heard from them since, and I don't want to talk about them. I honestly don't care what you believe and what you don't."

"And yet that's more words than you've ever said to me, daughter," Karen responded with a knowing smirk. "So, clearly, you care more than you want to admit."

"You really are just horrible," I said with a laugh. "Like, you're almost a comic book villain. When you were getting ready to incarnate on this earth, and people were lining up for souls and consciences, did you just skip that line?"

"I didn't call you here to fight with you." Karen turned away from me as if trying to get the ordinary toxicity that powered her under control. Or, at least, so it didn't show through so clearly. "I need your help. Well, I don't really need your help. We need to do something together. For both of us."

"Are you out of your mind? Why on earth would you think I would help you?"

"Because it's your fault Conrad Noble's dead."

SIXTEEN

"Sure. Of course. It was my fault entirely." My pronouncement was dripping with sarcasm. Karen looked at me as if trying to decide which angle to attack me from. Finally, she tossed her head, and with a sweep of her hand, she strode over to the bed. Spinning back to face me, she sat down primly and crossed her legs. "You haven't asked me anything about our family history, Fortuna. Anything about my motivations—"

"That's because I don't care about our family history. I know enough. And I definitely don't care about your motivations. I care about your results." I grabbed a metal chair and slung it aggressively across the highly polished floor until it came to rest directly across from her. Sitting down, I crossed my own legs and arms for good measure. "I never met Conrad Noble, didn't know the man. I highly doubt anything I did contributed to his death."

"And yet he wouldn't be dead if it weren't for you."

I ground my teeth in frustration. "Who killed him?"

"I have no idea."

"Then why would you think I had anything to do with his death?"

"I didn't say that you had anything directly to do with his death," my mother answered sharply. "I said it was your fault."

I had the distinct sense I was being toyed with. "You're playing word games. I'm not in the mood for word games."

"If you took some time to understand who I am, you would understand that this is no word game. At its core, the magic simply exerts pressure or influence on something intended to go one way when you want it to go another way. Yes?" she asked serenely as she poured water from a pitcher into a styrofoam cup. "Even your telepathy. You simply intercept thoughts and feelings that are not intended for anyone other than the person thinking or feeling them." My mother took a delicate sip of water. "Magic is, ultimately, just a powerful manipulation."

I wanted to get up and walk out of the room. I didn't need a magic lesson. Least of all from her.

But I couldn't.

I was sure Mom was toying with me, knew this moment was some brilliant performance she had practiced multiple times in her mind. An elliptical conversation would follow. One that would circle widely around the information I needed to know while she fed me agenda-laden observations about what she wanted me to believe.

I somehow had to break the circle, straighten it out into a line, and get her to tell me what I needed to know.

Even though I wasn't even sure what that was.

My face hardened. "And your point?"

"Our ancestor—our ultimate mother, if you will —knew this about magic. She knew even with magic, the Delphi coven could never stand up against the men that wanted this town for themselves. Despite being witches, we are not omnipotent. It wasn't just about magic versus weapons." Karen lifted her shoulders in a smooth gesture of nonchalance. "She knew that neither side could stand on its own without the other. And so she bound them together—"

"Are you trying to justify the witch that betrayed her coven?" I asked incredulously. "You think that what she did was right? You have to be kidding. She was not the good guy in this story."

"I think what she did was necessary for the time. And the women in the bottles never would've been there if they, too, had simply supported the town's move forward into the world."

Miss Bessie and Mary watched intently as my mother calmly explained the rationale of an oath-breaking witch over two hundred years in the ground. "Perhaps you should ask her direct questions, Fortuna," Miss Bessie suggested. "I have a feeling she's just going to keep pushing for you to see all this as a positive, not a negative."

I nodded once. "Why can't you see ghosts?" I asked her.

She looked at me in surprise. "How do you know I can't see them?"

"Because I can. And you can't. You can't see or hear them. Why?"

"You know I gained most of my power through binding others to me," my mother said in a muted tone. She looked off into space, her face soft as she remembered. "It's funny, the strangest places you'll find an idea. I got this one from a *Star Trek* film, believe it or not. The Borg Queen?" Without realizing I was doing it, I nodded. My mother took this is as a sign to continue. "I first used the dead to gain stronger powers, more potent energy. After all, the dead were dead. It's not like they needed any of their residual life force."

I recoiled. "You connected yourself to spirits?"

"Thanks to the curse on this town, it was like shooting fish in a barrel," she laughed menacingly. "They were all here, so many of them. Just milling about, confused as to why they couldn't leave. Mystic's End was so haunted you couldn't throw a rock in any direction in this town without hitting a ghost."

I frowned. "Where'd they all go? There are almost no ghosts here now."

She ignored my question. "Spiritual energy is powerful, but it wasn't enough. And controlling ghosts?" Karen shrugged again. "There's not much you can do with them. They make wonderful spies, of course. But if you really want to exert pressure with them? They're not that useful."

"So you switched from hooking up to ghosts to hooking up to live paranormals," I guessed.

"They were much more useful. I'm sure you realize that." My mother looked at me knowingly. "Your little boyfriend could tear the throat out of any mortal in seconds. You can't tell me that isn't part of his appeal for you."

"That isn't part of his appeal for me." My voice was suddenly harsh. I unfocused my eyes and stared into the spaces around my mother. Catching sight of several more cords connecting her to something, I contemplated snipping them again.

"It won't work," Karen muttered.

"What won't work?"

"The cord you're thinking about cutting," the older woman said with an impatient wave. "You don't think that's the only power I had in reserve, do you? Surely by now, you realize that I'm decades ahead of you. You don't know all my secrets, Fortuna. If you're going to make a move, be sure the step you take is the one you should be taking. You could make things worse for yourself." My mother paused ominously. "Or others."

There was an icy silence as we stared at each other.

I jumped up out of the chair. "I have to go to the restroom. I'll be back."

* * *

"What does she mean?"

I'd gone out the door to the visitor's hallway, circled around, and entered the monitoring room from the back way.

"Which part?" Chris asked me.

"Yeah, frankly, it's like y'all are talking in code," Beau Conroe said, scratching his head.

"Explain it to him when I'm back in there," I

told Chris. "What is she talking about? What other power is she talking about?" Chris squeezed my hand, and I jerked it away. He stared at me, his face concerned. "Look, I'm sorry, I just don't need to be soothed right now. I need answers. Do you know of any other way she gets her power?"

"Well, she's a witch, isn't she?" Clutterbuck said, looking back and forth between Chris and me. "Doesn't she just naturally have power?"

"Yes, she's a witch, but most witches don't have this much power. I lived in the paranormal world for a time, and even the most powerful witches there couldn't curse an entire town all at once and keep it going. Or force-control an army of paranormals. This is god-level power."

"Are you saying she's a god?" Conroe asked, his face growing pale.

"No, I'm saying she's really working hard to be on that level, but she's not," I answered. I tapped the desk impatiently with my fingers until Chris looked up at me. "You don't know what she's talking about, do you?"

"I don't, Fortuna. I'm sorry. I wish I did. This is the first I've ever heard of her being able to connect with ghosts and use them for her own ends." I could see his regret—and his frustration—that he didn't have answers. Chris grabbed my hand for a second time and squeezed with his steel vampire strength.

This time I didn't pull away and squeezed back. "Thank you," he said simply and then let go.

"I'm sorry, I'm just frustrated." I paced the polished floor and thought. "Okay, so what we know. Karen is a descendant of the witch that betrayed the Delphi coven. To give the town over to the man that showed up and wanted it, she cast a curse on her other coven sisters that if they or their descendants fought the invaders, they would die." I stopped and turned as if I had an epiphany. "And they wound up in witch bottles so they wouldn't haunt the town, and so they would continue powering the shield around the town. Which is almost gone."

"What if none of them had ever died in that manner?" Clutterbuck asked.

"Well, then you wouldn't need the curse on the town anymore, right?" I guessed. "Maybe it only kept going as long as there were witches."

"There's no curse on the town," Beau Conroe interjected, frowning.

"There's definitely, without a doubt, a curse on the town," I disagreed.

"No," Conroe argued. "That's the whole point of the church. The church rituals make sure there's a bubble of protection on the town. There can't be a curse. I mean, we would know it. Well, they would know it. The churchgoers."

I turned and stared at the detective. "What do you mean? How would they know it?"

"Well, the ball glows." He shared this bit of information without a trace of irony and with no further explanation. "The ball?" He looked from face to face to face, seeing the confusion but not understanding. "The crystal ball that the men take care of. The ball is important because it shows that the town is still under spiritual protection. After the service is over, it glows white, and everyone knows the town is protected."

"The selenite ball," I said and shifted to look at Chris.

"Just like the selenite Martin's mother is encased in," he countered.

"How did the church get the ball?" I asked Beau.

He swallowed and shifted uncomfortably. Looking up, he finally responded.

"Your mother gave it to them. At the church's founding."

* * *

"I want an answer. Why can't you see ghosts?" I asked her as I stormed into the room.

"That must've been a heck of a bathroom break," Mary murmured.

My mother stared at me, shocked at the change in my demeanor. "As I told you, initially, I would connect to ghosts. Obviously, being connected to so many spirits is difficult. Once I had enough power, I removed my ability to see and hear them. They would beg to be set free, and...well, obviously, I would not do that. All I needed was their power. I had other methods to spy on people by then." She shrugged.

There was something here. I could feel it. Something important.

"Tell me about the selenite ball you gave the church," I demanded.

A slow smile spread across her face. "Outstanding, Fortuna. I was wondering when you would understand. Now you know why I need you to go to the church."

I blinked.

I didn't know why she needed me to go to the church.

But she obviously thought I did, so I played along.

"I understand why," I lied, "but I don't understand what you need me to do. How am I supposed to do it?"

"I'm shocked you agree so easily." My mother stood up, her eyes narrowing. "Though I doubt you're doing it for me. You probably feel sorry for those poor souls. I'm just lucky your compassion will benefit me. With no witch, their rituals are almost useless and astrally projecting? It didn't work." She rolled her eyes and stepped toward her television, frowning as she examined the severed cord. "Of course, it could also be your stupid binding spell."

"Of course, I feel sorry for the churchgoers. You've convinced them an army of paranormals is coming to attack their town in retribution for something that only you remember happened."

My mother lifted her head and stared at me, her eyes glittering.

"I don't think she's talking about the churchgoers, Fortuna," Mary told me in a strangled voice.

"Mary, what do you know?" Miss Bessie asked harshly.

"I know nothing, Mom. At least not for sure," Mary answered. She glared at Karen in disbelief. "But Fortuna severed all the cords on her mother several months ago. And yet now there are more. She's like an energy vampire, but from everything she said? It sounds like she can only pull from two kinds of beings. Ghosts, and paranormals."

"What are you saying?" I asked.

"Who are you talking to?" my mother asked, her voice edgy.

"Mary Wilcox," I told her.

"That tart?" With casual ease, Karen turned and cast her eyes around the room. "Just another one of the women Marty Salvatore thought he could control. Mary, you'll be happy to know that he completely forgot you. I made sure of that. Thanks to your magical lessons, in fact."

"If I had hands? They'd be around your neck right now," Mary seethed.

"It must thrill her to be watching me: me, the person who got everything that she wanted. The money, the magical power, the man," Karen said with a cheerful smugness. "You were instrumental, Mary, in helping me achieve my ends. I should really thank you. I would thank you, in fact." Her eyes suddenly looked fierce. "If you weren't dead."

"Can't you hit her with a fire-bolt or something?" Mary asked me.

"I got them all out of the way. Mary, Anna. All of them," my mother continued as Miss Bessie tried to calm her daughter down. "All the women that thought they could stand in my way. In the end, none of them could."

"All so you could be with Martin's father?" I asked her.

"Well, look at what it got me!"

"Mother, you're in jail!"

"Temporary setback." She waved her

circumstances away as if they were a fly that had buzzed too close. "Once you go to the church and you help those yokels perform the ceremony on the crystal ball, my power will return. Well, enough of it, I can leave this ill-appointed cell without a single legal entanglement. Once that's done, I can rebuild my empire—hopefully with you at my side. Once you understand."

"Your empire?"

"Yes, my empire! You don't think those men thought up all of this on their own, do you?" Karen asked me. "I brought Martin Salvatore up from nothing, from a petty street criminal to a titan!"

"And the key to it all is that crystal ball?"

"Yes," she told me, her eyes wide. "It is the last of my adjunct power, my tie to Anna's life force, and once we get it back, daughter, you and I will be able to—"

There it was.

"So, you keep all of your adjunct power in that crystal ball?" I asked once more, just to be sure.

"The power's not in the ball, Fortuna. The ghosts are in the ball, and I pulled my power from the ghosts, and Anna Salvi."

Blank faces.

On me, on Miss Bessie. On Mary.

Then puzzled faces.

Then horror.

"There are ghosts in that crystal ball?" Miss Bessie asked.

"But it's so...well, I guess we were in bottles, so..." Mary looked shocked.

"I just want to make sure I'm absolutely clear, Mom," I asked, trying to sound as helpful as I could. "You need me to do a ritual with the church because there are ghosts locked in the crystal ball." She nodded excitedly, pleased I was finally getting it. "And this ritual does what, exactly?"

"It keeps them from degrading, of course. The town has to remember their ancestors, to keep their memory alive." My mother stared into my eyes. "If they don't, the souls will degrade and then just disappear. Degraded souls have a lot less power."

I blinked.

I blinked again.

I swallowed. "How many souls are in the crystal ball, Mom?"

Karen stared at me with a combination of relief and exhilaration. "Why, all of them, Fortuna. The entire town. Everyone who's died since the curse was cast."

Miss Bessie stared at my mother, her face outraged, as in appalled silence we tried to absorb what we had just heard.

SEVENTEEN

We all jumped at the sound of metal slamming against the cinder block—even the ghosts.

A bellow followed the jarring sound, courtesy of a furious Chief Clutterbuck bursting through the door. "Did you shove my wife in a crystal ball?" the chief roared, marching up to the bars. Chris followed him closely, his face tight with concern. "Karen, did you imprison my wife in a crystal ball?" He glowered contemptuously at her. "Answer me!"

Detective Beau Conroe crept in slowly. His face was pale, and he looked around with a sort of dumb amazement—as if he couldn't quite believe all that he'd just observed.

"Did I personally imprison your wife?" My

mother tossed her head casually. It seemed intended to infuriate Clutterbuck. "Your wife—well, everyone really—was imprisoned in this town before I drew my first breath, Terry." The self-congratulatory way she announced this turned my stomach. "I just made their prison ball a little smaller. That's all. They are ghosts, after all. It's not like they need much room. None of this is because of me. I just took advantage of the situation."

Clutterbuck looked enraged—and overwhelmed. I sensed the confusion churning within him, thoughts racing through his mind and being discarded almost in the same moment. The man had an overwhelming desire to rescue his wife —and the overpowering feeling he was helpless to do anything against these forces he didn't understand.

"Take a breath, Chief," I whispered. "We'll figure this out."

He didn't respond.

He didn't even look at me.

"Are you telling me...are you telling me the church has been working against the town all this time?" Beau Conroe asked with glassy-eyed horror. "All these years, you've roped my mother into doing these things, thinking she was on the side of the righteous, and yet...she's effectively been a prison guard." Conroe squeezed his hands into fists. "A prison guard for people you are exploiting. People she cared about. Members of our family."

"Dead people...I was exploiting dead people." Karen tilted her head. "Are dead people really people? I mean, if you stop to think about it, they aren't really people anymore, are they? Nothing has happened to anyone in town that's alive, Detective. You've all had your little small town existence unencumbered. It's just your death I interfere with." My mother nodded as if her agreement was all that mattered and then turned to me. "And thank you for violating our privacy. I see you're not grown-up enough for me to trust you." She gave a dismissive wave of her hand. "All I asked for was a conversation with my daughter, a private one. You couldn't even do that."

"Why on earth would you think you could trust me with this garbage?" I responded with disgust. "Right now, I am mortified that I'm related to you in any capacity. You seem to get savage enjoyment out of screwing people over, out of exploiting them, out of getting away with it. You are a horrible human being!"

"Watch yourself, daughter. Haven't you heard about apples and how they don't fall far from trees?"

"Shut up!" I shouted, my head pounding. Stars sparked in front of my eyes.

Everything about my mother was infuriating me. That she gave birth to me, that she gave me away like a lucky rabbit's foot. Somewhere in my brain, I knew Chris had stepped beside me, but I could barely feel the pressure from his hand.

"Fortuna Delphi," my mother scolded, but my shout stopped anything else she would say to me.

"You are severely mentally ill, or you're twisted, or you're just plain broken—"

"Careful, daughter," Karen said as she stepped toward me, her palm held toward me. "Once you get over the shock of finding all this out, I'm sure you'll see that my way is far better than—"

"Shut up! Shut up!" I shouted, my voice shaking with blistering anger. The sparks before my eyes grew bigger. "Undo this! You can't do this to people!" The room felt frozen as if I'd suspended it in time. I could sense no one else other than my mother, and what I was sensing from her would haunt me for the rest of my life. If I was fire and fury, she was ice cold.

My mother reached through the bars to grab my hand. "Fortuna—"

"Don't touch me!" I shouted again, shoving her hand away with every thought, every feeling, every emotion I had.

Things must've happened fast.

I mean, looking back on it, I know it was fast.

It didn't feel fast.

The first thing I noticed was a rushing sound in my ears, like the pounding surf at high tide. My mother's face looked uncertain for the first time, her eyes wide as she stared at me in dismay—but then it disappeared from view as if enveloped by fog. The last thing I saw was her hand still clasping mine.

Then there was the light. It was so bright. Almost blinding. As if the sparks that popped and crackled in front of my eyes supernova'd, then shot forward with almost comic exaggeration toward my mother.

The crack of energy was almost deafening.

Chris, of course, dove at me to shield me from whatever was happening. "Are you all right?" he asked me as we lay together on the floor, his body protecting mine.

"I'm fine," I told him, shivering. I was cold. It was as if all the heat had just fled my body. That the ice cold vampire's body was several degrees cooler than mine wasn't exactly helping.

"Are you sure?" he asked. He turned my face toward him and stared deep into my eyes.

I blushed with embarrassment while nodding. "I'm okay. What happened, though? Was that me?" He didn't answer. "I think that was maybe me."

Then I heard a dog bark.

* * *

The four of us stood outside of the cell and stared in.

The greyhound looked back at us, its soft eyes calm.

Every once in a while, the dog blinked.

"You turned her into a dog," Clutterbuck said, his face pale with open disbelief. "Fortuna Delphi, I think you turned your mother into a dog. How on earth did you turn your mother into a dog?"

The greyhound wagged its tail and barked again.

I didn't answer.

Detective Conroe looked queasy and stumbled toward a wastebasket. Unattractive sounds followed.

"Well, I guess that takes care of her," Mary Wilcox said, her words reverberating with a sense of triumph. "I've studied a lot of magic, and I'm almost sure that greyhounds cannot cast spells. All's well that ends well, I suppose."

"I think your ending pronouncement may be premature," Chris told Mary.

"What about Gideon?" I asked her. "He can send telepathic images."

"Only to you. He's your familiar. Different situation," Miss Bessie responded. The ghost floated down toward the dog and waved her hand in front of its face. It barked and stuck its wet nose out to sniff her hand—looking surprised as its nose floated through it. "She can see ghosts now." The older woman stood back up. "That shows to me she doesn't have so much as a drop of magic anymore. She cast that spell on herself, the one that blocked her ability to see us. It did not go with her into her new species. She's done. Finally."

"What are you all saying?" Clutterbuck asked.

I told him.

"Her new species? Her new species?" Clutterbuck asked, his eyes blinking rapidly to clear the glaze of confusion. "You're going to leave her a dog? You can't leave a human being as a dog. Not even that one."

"Well, she can," Mary quipped with unconcealed amusement. "She's done it before."

"Mary," Miss Bessie frowned with disapproval.

"What? You know you were thinking it."

I didn't answer Chief Clutterbuck. I wasn't sure what to say.

"Fortuna is not sure how she accomplishes transmogrification," Chris offered to the chief helpfully. "This is only the second time she's done it, and as far as I'm aware, she's not yet learned how to reverse it." I nodded in agreement. Chris looked down at the greyhound. It was sitting quietly and gazing from person to person. "Unfortunately, Karen will have to stay a dog for the foreseeable future."

"Is that really so bad?" Mary asked the chief with a puzzled frown, but Clutterbuck could not see or hear her.

"For once, you and I agree," Miss Bessie nodded at her daughter. "Normally, I'd tear Fortuna here a new one for not having control of her magic, for letting her emotions get the best of her. Heck, for just being downright dangerous." Bessie waved her hands in front of the dog again, and the dog barked back happily. "In this case, though, well done. Honestly, Fortuna, I think Karen looks happier than she's ever looked."

I pouted in silence.

Chris caught me in his arms. "Fortuna, it's going to be fine."

I spat out a very unladylike epithet and looked down in embarrassment.

"Fortuna," Chris whispered in that low, sexy voice only I could hear. "I know it was an accident, and I know you're a little embarrassed, but I think Miss Bessie may be right. We were having a lot of trouble undoing what Karen had done. I know you didn't mean to do it, but now that's done? It may be the best thing that could've happened."

"There is so much I didn't find out," I replied in

a whisper into his granite-like chest. My voice sounded flat, weary. "I wanted to find out who our —Dalida's and my—birth father was. Or is. If he's still alive. Why she had the three of us. I mean, why three? Was there a reason? Was Angie more than a means to an end? And who were her parents? Why was she the way she was?" As I complained, I suddenly realized none of these questions seemed important—until I knew I might never get the answers.

"You are a combination of everything you know and everything you have chosen to become." Slowly, deliberately, Chris pulled back and tilted my head up with one hand. There was no doubt in his eyes. No fear that his girlfriend might turn him into a dog in a fit of pique. "Those answers would not have changed you. The damage she could have done to you? That might have."

"As much as I have sympathy toward you, Fortuna, for the emotional moment you're having with your boyfriend, I'd like to point out that we are not alone here. How am I supposed to explain the disappearance of a prisoner awaiting trial?" Chief Clutterbuck asked the group in stunned disbelief. "For that matter, how am I supposed to explain why there's a greyhound in this jail?" Suddenly, his eyes grew wide. "This whole room, this whole situation, is being recorded!"

Chris kissed me quickly on the cheek and shot out of the room so fast no one's eyes could follow.

After a few seconds of silence, Clutterbuck cleared his throat. "He's not going to drink the guards, is he?"

The sound of Beau Conroe's retching resumed a few seconds after that.

* * *

"I have taken care of the recording," Chris said as soon as he reappeared. "The camera and audio into this room will have to be repaired, Chief Clutterbuck. My apologies, but there was no other way."

"The dog?" Clutterbuck asked, gesturing toward the reddish-colored dog. It was, at that moment, excitedly attempting to squeeze its wide-barreled chest through the bars. The chief paused for a moment and then looked at me. "Is that a dog? I mean, does she know she was a human and was just turned into a dog? Or is Karen just gone?"

"I don't know. Ella Grayson—"

"I thought Ella Grayson got on a plane and got out of Dodge?" Clutterbuck asked me, his eyes narrowing with suspicion.

"Well, she almost made it to her car, and I think she was going to the airport," I told him sheepishly.

"I can stop having anybody look for Ella Grayson?" the chief asked with irritation.

"You can."

"I hope we don't have a murderous dog running around eating people."

"Nope. I'm well acquainted with Ella as a dog," I told him. "She's made somebody an excellent pet." I decided not to explain his daughter's dog was the murderous fugitive. Watching me turn my mother into a dog was probably enough excitement for one night.

"Speaking of, my two questions still stand. How am I supposed to explain Karen White's disappearance, and how am I supposed to explain a dog suddenly appearing in the jail?"

"Can we just fake a breakout?" Chris asked, his eyebrow raised. "We just disabled the audio and visual equipment. There will be no fingerprints. We can unlock the cell door and leave it open. After a search, you can bring the tunnel underneath the police department to everyone's attention." Chris looked down at the greyhound. "I can sneak the dog out using the tunnel for now."

"And bring it where?" Beau asked with distaste. "Don't we need her to free the town from the crystal ball prison?"

"I don't know," Chris said, turning toward me. "Do we?"

"I don't think so," I told him, shaking my head. "She doesn't have any magic anymore. It's going to be up to me—well, probably me and my sisters—to figure out a way to get everybody out." I looked at Beau Conroe. "I need that bottle. You've seen what's going on here, enough to understand what we're trying to do. That bottle is another prison, and someone's trapped in it. I need to get them out."

"There's someone in that tiny bottle?" Conroe gasped.

"Yes, just like there's apparently an entire town full of people stuck in the crystal ball. Anyway, that has to be the next step because the witch bottles' witches were feeding the curse. The curse was partially the boundary. If the overall curse comes down," I said, thinking it through as I talked, "the parts of the magic that are this colonial curse thing should be done with. Then we only have to deal with the magic Karen herself cast to imprison the ghosts in the crystal ball."

"This is enough to make a man drink," Clutterbuck muttered.

"There is an urgency to this now, so we need to pick a plan." Chris looked at his watch. "I don't want Fortuna and her sisters going into that church without me, and I'm going to run out of moonlight in about eight hours."

Conroe nodded. "I can get you the bottle. It's in

the evidence locker. What else do we need to do?" Beau Conroe asked nervously.

"Pepper and Ollie are already at the church. I'll call Martin and have him bring Angie. Chris, you call Dalida. She and Gabe can meet us."

Chris nodded, then thought for a moment. Swinging his head to look at the ghosts, he said, "Miss Bessie? Can you and Mary go get the ghosts? You all should be there, too. You may see things that even we cannot."

"We'll be there as fast as we can gather everyone," Miss Bessie nodded. She and Mary turned toward the back wall and disappeared.

"One thing none of this made clear," Clutterbuck said, then he sighed in frustration.

"What's that?" I asked.

"Why was Conrad Noble killed? Who put the magic on his house, on the evidence room here? If it wasn't Beau—"

"It might have been me," Beau interrupted, his eyes downcast.

"What do you mean?" Chris asked him.

"Karen gave me these little dolls. Crude little things—"

"Poppets," I told him. "They are made to represent a person. A witch can cast a spell on a poppet, and the doll stands in for the person." I frowned. "She cast magic specifically against me, then?" Beau Conroe looked like he wanted to do anything other than answer my question, but finally, he nodded.

I glanced over at the dog. It stared back at me with unapologetic directness.

"Well, that gives me hope, I guess."

"Hope?" Clutterbuck asked, confused.

"If she was targeting me specifically to keep me away from anything having to do with that crystal ball?" I told Clutterbuck, my eyes still glued to the dog that used to be my mother. "Maybe I'm the key to freeing this town and ending this curse once and for all."

EIGHTEEN

The deep night had fallen even darker with a vast opaque gloom. A fog bank had rolled in despite there being no chill in the air, giving the church a haunted look.

And speaking of the church in a small town at almost midnight? It seemed to be the hopping place to hang on a Wednesday. I counted at least twenty cars in the parking lot. A ridiculously high number, one would think, for the middle of the week, deep into the night when most citizens should be home sleeping.

Unless they knew we were coming.

"Should we go in?" Chief Clutterbuck asked me. The chief, the detective, and I stood beside his police car, waiting for the others. When I didn't respond, I sensed his gaze drift down toward my hand, where the witch bottle Beau Conroe had given me was clutched tightly in my fingers.

It had apparently been in the evidence room all along, enchanted, so no one who intended to give it to me could see it.

How to get around the spell?

Beau Conroe intended to give it to Chief Clutterbuck as he grabbed it.

Chief Clutterbuck then handed it to me.

That was all it took.

"I think we should wait for everybody," I murmured finally.

"Okay, we can do that." More staring at the bottle in my hand.

I turned. "What's on your mind, Chief?"

"Do you uncork that thing in the church or something?" he asked. "Why not just open it?"

"I can't open it myself." I turned away and resumed staring at each stained glass window, hoping to get a sense of what was going on inside the building. There were no shadows, no movement. If there were people in there, they were staying out of sight. Hopefully, Pepper and Ollie would have more information. She told me she would keep checking for our arrival, and as soon as she saw us, they would sneak out to meet us.

"Pardon me," Beau asked, a bleary-eyed

weariness audible in his tone. "But if there's a curse that's been on Mystic's End for several hundred years, and you're supposed to be the witch that breaks that curse and frees the town, shouldn't you be able to at least uncork a bottle?"

I turned and stared at him.

"That was a little rude, Detective," Chief Clutterbuck admonished the younger man. "Though," he said, turning toward me, "a legitimate question if you really stop and think about it. Why can't you uncork the bottle?"

"We need two magical users. I guess it's like a circuit. One person holds the bottle, and the other person pulls up the cork."

Both men gave off befuddled energy. I could have stopped and explained the magical concept of a closed circuit to both of them. Unfortunately, my mind was occupied with trying to develop a nonconfrontational—and creative—way to march into a church holding twenty ideologues. So I could explain to them that their faith was a lie.

"There are Pepper and Ollie," I said, spotting the two rushing out a side door and hurrying toward the parking lot. "Maybe they'll have more information about what's going on in there."

"Is that the assistant coroner?" Beau Conroe choked out. His mind exploded with panic over what type of paranormal Ollie might be and what he might've been doing with the town's dead bodies.

"You're not going to throw up again, are you?" Chief Clutterbuck asked him sharply. "You're looking kind of green again, and I just bought these shoes. Pull it together, Conroe. You're supposed to be one of Mystic End's finest. Try to act like it." He blasted Conroe with a look of warning.

The detective swallowed and nodded.

"Hey," Pepper said as she bounced up to the three of us, Ollie right on her heels. "I didn't quite get what the heck was going on. Can you explain it to me?" She elbowed her boyfriend and winked.

"Which part?" I asked in a flat tone—knowing the teasing was inescapable.

"Woof," the reporter responded, radiant amusement coloring her cheeks pink.

"I can't believe you're actually getting a laugh out of this situation."

"I didn't laugh. Well, I did laugh when you called and told me what you'd done," she admitted. "I made absolutely sure I disconnected my cell phone, and the call ended before I started laughing, though. I didn't want to hurt your feelings." Pepper smiled sweetly at me as if she was trying to placate me.

I waged an internal debate with myself on

whether she would get me angry enough to turn her into a dog. "What changed?" I asked.

"I mean, you have to admit, Fortuna—it is kind of funny."

"I doubt Karen finds it very funny," Ollie pointed out. The biker's voice wasn't quite a reprimand, but I was a little startled that he seemed concerned. "Look, I know you didn't do it on purpose," he blurted, catching my expression. "I'm not passing judgment or anything, I get it. But I don't think this is something we should laugh about."

"I feel positively chastised," said Pepper as she turned and stuck her tongue out at Ollie.

He just rolled his eyes.

"Truthfully, I don't know that I'd agree with you, Oliver," Chief Clutterbuck told Ollie Kane. "It may be because greyhounds always look like they're smiling, or Karen is just relieved she no longer has to do all that plotting and planning to destroy people. Whatever it is, though, the dog looked pretty content."

"Where is it?" Pepper asked, her eyes sparkling. "I have to see it."

"She's not here. The vampire is bringing her the long way." Clutterbuck jerked his head toward the tree line. "We had to sneak her out of jail. Didn't know how to explain a greyhound on the women's block."

"Yeah, I can see that," Ollie answered. "So, do you want to know what we found?"

"Let's wait." I glanced around at the tree line. "Better to explain this to everyone all at once."

The five of us stood quietly next to the police cruiser and waited.

* * *

The ghosts arrived first.
      And they were nervous.

"Everyone's here," Spike said, his spiky blue hair coiffed, his blue jeans and button-down shirt imaginary-ironed. "I have to tell you, though, everyone is really freaking out. You know this is what everyone wanted, right?" He pulled back, his eyes searching the spectral crowd milling about on the church's front lawn. "Even so, none of them are really sure what's going to happen." Spike turned back to me. "What is going to happen?"

"I wish I knew," I said as I met his gaze. "First, we'll free whoever they locked up in this bottle."

"Do you want to do that now?" Chris asked as he walked up, carrying...um, my mother.

"Holy moly, Fortuna, that's—"

Before Spike could finish his statement, the

nearly thirty ghosts milling about turned and gasped.

"I told you we should have told them first," Miss Bessie said as she floated to the front. "The dog looks completely different to us. They know it ain't right."

"We didn't have time to stop and give these women that information, Mother," Mary said incredulously. "You always want to stop and talk about things, and we didn't have time to talk about things. Now, we're all standing here doing nothing, and Fortuna can tell the ghosts whatever it is she wants to tell them. They can ask whatever it is they want to ask. Now, we have time to talk about things, Mother." Mary placed her hands on her hips. "We didn't before."

"And you think I talk too much," Miss Bessie deadpanned.

Mary pointedly ignored her response.

"Are Gabe and Dalida on their way?" I asked Miss Bessie. She nodded. I turned to Chris again. "How about Martin and Angie?"

"Will be here shortly. Do you want to wait for them, or should we do the bottle now?"

I glanced at the other ghosts. "No one else that we freed was aggressive or bad or anything, so we may as well get it done now." Chris nodded and carefully placed the greyhound he was carrying down on its feet. Holding out the leash to Pepper, he relinquished control of the dog to a woman that could barely contain her laughter. "I'm glad you're finding this amusing," Chris told her.

"I'm a little alarmed you're finding it amusing," Ollie muttered.

"Oh, hush, I get my laughs where I can." Pepper kneeled down in front of the dog and looked into its eyes. "You don't look like a psychopathic crazy lady. No, you don't," she cooed as she reached up to scratch the dog's ears. "Do you like that? Do you like that, crazy psychopathic lady? Who's the psycho? Who's the adorable little psycho? Yes, you are." The dog barked happily and wagged its tail as Pepper scratched her. "Can I keep her?"

"My life is so unbelievably weird," I whispered, staring at the scene in what might—might—be a growing sense of shock. My eyes teared up unexpectedly at the strange scene: my closest friend playing with the dog that was, in truth, the woman who so devastated my life. Both happy. A scene that should engender feelings of joy was now a vision producing conflict in me. Churning emotions.

Guilt.

Anger.

After everything Karen White had done, why should she be happy?

"Fortuna," Chris said, drawing me into his arms. "Don't fall apart now."

"None of this is right," I protested, tensing in his embrace. "She doesn't get to be happy. She's a monster. This isn't right."

"None of this has been right for a long time. You're getting 'right' back for most people." He glanced at my mother. "Even for her, maybe. This is a good thing. Something you should be proud of."

"Proud? Are you kidding me? She doesn't deserve it," I told him, my voice hollow.

Chris pulled back and tipped my head up to him. He'd done it so often that just the touch of his finger on my chin caused me to feel a deep connection to him. Seconds later, our eyes met. "Was your goal to stop the damage she was causing or was your goal retribution for the damage she's caused?" he asked me simply. "Those two things are not the same."

I stared into his eyes, not wanting to answer. I knew what my answer should be, and I knew what my answer probably was. I didn't want to admit to him what I felt.

But I also didn't want to lie.

After a few seconds, the vampire's expression softened. "I don't judge you for not telling me the 'right' answer immediately. We both know what that is. The one that makes you seem like a selfless martyr unaffected by some desire to lash out at this woman who hurt you so deeply. It's only natural." He took a deep breath for effect. "But love, I have to tell you unequivocally—you must let it go. It can poison you. Before this night is over, you will have freed everyone imprisoned by your ancestors. You will have unlocked the dead. And you will have freed those of us who lived in fear of what Karen would do if she gained power again. I am sure of it." He tilted his head. "See that. Feel that. Know that. And let go any anger over what she's done. You'll be the better for it."

"You know, for a vampire, you kind of sound like a hippie," I told him as I pulled away.

He looked at me with sympathy etched on his face. Such a bizarre thing. He was such a fierce creature. A killer, really. Designed to be. Who would have ever thought that a vampire—a vampire —could be so softhearted? Chris stared at me patiently, but he didn't respond to my taunt. If he could read me, I could also read him.

That all-knowing expression, the one he wore when he was sure I was trying to push him away.

The quiet, patient head tilt he always had while he waited for me to get over myself.

"I'm sorry, I know I'm doing that pushing away thing. But I heard you. I promise." Chris picked up on the weariness in my voice, and he pulled me close again, silently, and just held me. After what seemed like hours, I whispered, "I really love you, you know that?"

Slowly, he pulled back to look me in the eye. His eyebrow was raised. "I did. Even though you've never said it to me before. But I did know. I could feel it." He dropped the eyebrow and smiled. "I'm sorry. That sounded like a recrimination, and that wasn't my intent at all. I love that you finally felt comfortable enough to say it."

I stiffened defensively at his response—and that he didn't say it back. "Look, just because I'm not some gooshy girl that just, like, vomits affection all over you doesn't mean I don't love you." I rolled my eyes. "Jeez."

The smile faded. "I sincerely apologize again," he said. I looked away, not sure how to respond. After a few moments, Chris added, "I'm sorry I misspoke." I gave an exaggerated sigh. "Fortuna, you're doing the—"

"Defensive thing again, I know." I turned back toward him, staring for a few moments. Then I deliberately pushed away the negative feelings I had ushered into the moment. It was a special moment. And I did love him. With my whole heart.

"I will never judge you," he responded simply.

"Me, neither," I promised.

"And I love you, too."

Then he kissed me—a nice long kiss.

That stopped as soon as we heard Beau Conroe retching.

* * *

"She's really that dog?" Dalida asked, staring at the greyhound in horror. Gideon strained against the leash in her hand as he tried to sniff the newcomer. Karen was already playing with Bella, Angie's greyhound, who'd arrived just moments before with Martin and Angie.

"I can't believe you turned Karen into a dog!" Angie laughed, aghast. "This is just hysterical. And I thought what I could do was cool! I guess that fairytale about turning a frog into a prince or a prince into a frog or whatever has some basis in fact, huh? Wow, you turned mommy dearest into a greyhound!" My younger sister laughed uproariously as if it was the funniest joke she'd ever heard. "Well, I'll be!"

"I have to say, Fortuna, I'm thrilled I never made you angrier than I did. I didn't know you could do such a thing," Martin Salvi, Angie's boyfriend, observed with amazement. "I'm delighted, as furious as you've been at me, you didn't do it to me."

"Well, it's not like she hasn't done it before,"

Pepper said, pointing to Angie's greyhound Bella. "That's Ella Grayson! Or, well, it used to be Ella Grayson."

"Pepper!" I shouted and cast a furious glare in her direction.

"What are you talking about?" Angie asked, looking back and forth between Pepper and me. As if she could sense Dalida, who was standing behind her, moving back to avoid the line of fire, she whirled on our sister. "Where are you going, and why do you look so guilty? Dalida Dodd, tell me what's going on!"

"Fortuna did it," Dalida blurted out quickly, pointing toward me. "I didn't even live here then. It's not my fault."

"Fortuna Delphi, if you don't want me to punch you in the nose, you better explain yourself!"

I opened my mouth and then closed it. Opened it again and then sighed. "I didn't know how to tell you. I barely knew you when I realized you'd adopted that dog, and then we found we were sisters, and then we got close, and then..." I exhaled forcefully, and my shoulders slumped. "I'm sorry, Angie, I should've told you. I just didn't know how."

"We all told her she should tell you," Pepper agreed with a vociferous nod. "Didn't we, guys?"

Angie stared at Pepper. "Wait a minute. You all

knew?" she asked, her exaggerated southern belle accent burned away by the fury in her voice.

"Um." Pepper looked around for help.

"Some of us were aware, yes," Dalida answered quietly.

"I had no idea, baby doll, and I am absolutely appalled by your friends. That they never told you? Horrible, just horrible," Clutterbuck said with an authoritative toss of his head. "I can't believe they kept something like that from you."

"Weren't you the one that didn't tell her Karen was her mother?" I asked quietly. "Terry?" I added sarcastically for good measure.

"That wasn't very nice," Chris murmured, but he could barely suppress a smirk.

"Don't we have other things we need to do right now?" Clutterbuck asked haughtily. The big man crossed his arms. "Why don't y'all quit yapping and uncork that damn bottle so we can get on with this?"

"We are not done talking about this," Angie told me fiercely as she stepped away with one last glare.

I swallowed and held out the bottle toward Chris. Like all the others, the bottle uncorked, and mist poured from the mouth in a dreamy waterfall. It spread out on the asphalt. Those that could see it stepped back and watched.

Slowly, undoubtedly, a woman's form rose up and then solidified.

Or, well, solidified as much as mist to a ghost would solidify.

She smiled a friendly smile at me. "Thank you," the freed specter said in a quiet voice with a nod. "I knew you would get to me eventually, but I must admit the wait was a bit longer than I would've preferred." The woman, dressed in reasonably modern clothing, turned and gazed at Angie. Her face grew sad even though she smiled. "What a beautiful woman you grew up to be."

Angie watched, unseeing, and waited.

"And you." The ghost turned and stepped in front of Chief Clutterbuck.

I couldn't help but notice they were so mismatched. He was a tall, thick man. Muscled and big-boned, like a fighter. The woman was short and slight, her head only reaching his chest. "I heard you speak to me. Every time. I heard you through the marigolds you planted on my grave." She smiled up at the gruff lawman. "I so looked forward to Sundays. I don't think you ever missed one."

Dalida and I stared at each other.

"Who is it?" Angie asked. She looked back and forth between our gobsmacked expressions.

"It's your mother," Chris informed Angie. He glanced toward Chief Clutterbuck, who remained expressionless, unaware of what was happening in front of him.

"Wait, I thought Fortuna turned her into a dog—"

"Not Karen," Chris explained gently as Angie's bewildered expression froze on her face. "The last bottle? The last ghost, I believe, is Tara Clutterbuck. The mother that raised you. The wife of your father."

Chief Clutterbuck's face turned ashen. Then he pushed Detective Beau Conroe aside and raced toward the grass.

Where he threw up.

NINETEEN

"Do you think he's going to be okay?" Pepper asked, an uncommonly serious look of concern on her face. Dalida, Pepper, and I stood off to the side as Angie and her father talked privately with one another. Hovering behind them both, unseen? Tara Clutterbuck, newly freed from her bottle. "I don't think I've ever seen him so freaked out. I know I've never seen him throw up." She tilted her head and looked up. "Well, there was that one Fourth of July picnic, but I think that was food poisoning."

"He'll be fine. You, on the other hand, have some explaining to do," I told Pepper with an accusatory glare. "What on earth were you thinking, telling Angie about the dog in the middle of all this? Do you honestly not think before you open your mouth? I swear, I sometimes think you just—"

"I thought that by the time this night is over, that her dog used to be human is going to be the least of her issues. It seemed the best time to slip it in." Pepper ran her hands through her hair and then firmly placed her hands on her hips. "Look, I know you all think I just bumble through life spewing out whatever thought flips through my brain, but I don't. I went into journalism because secrets are toxic," she said, pointing toward the church. "Those people are about to find out they've been imprisoning Grandma for decades. Should we not tell them just because it's going to be tough for them to handle?"

"I didn't say that. And you're changing the subject," I argued.

"I'm not. I know everyone thinks I have boundary issues, that I don't think before I speak. You're wrong." Pepper glanced at Dalida, her face animated. "The two of you are twins, and you didn't even know it until you were well in your thirties. I open my mouth, and I say things people should know because people should know them. That's it. Because secrets are toxic. I didn't blurt it out because I wasn't thinking. I blurted it out because you should have told her two months ago."

Pepper tossed her head. "The three of you are living together. You're supposed to be sisters."

I stared.

"Why didn't you just talk to Fortuna before saying something?" Dalida asked her.

"I've said multiple times you all needed to tell her. Both of you. I've said it to both of you. Multiple times."

"Me?" Dalida asked, surprised.

"You're her sister, too. You knew the secret, too. You kept it from Angie the same as Fortuna."

Dalida looked like she would argue, but then she sighed. "You're right. I can't argue with you. But I also feel I have a point, as well. You should have taken us aside and had a serious talk with us if you were that concerned."

"I know we don't know each other very well, Dalida, but I don't really waste serious heart to heart talks trying to explain to people things I know they know already. If you get my drift." Pepper glanced over her shoulder to check on Angie and the chief and then turned back. "You both knew it wasn't right to keep it from her. What was I supposed to say to you? You knew."

Although I was the person who would free the town from a multi-century curse, my nearest and dearest were calling me on my stuff this evening.

Shouldn't the town savior get a break on the minor stuff?

"No," Pepper said as if she read my mind.

"Are you a telepath now?"

"I don't have to be telepathic to read your expression. By the way," Pepper asked, changing her tone to change the subject. "Since you opened that bottle up, does that mean the ghosts can get out of Mystic's End now?"

"Hopefully," I said, turning my head and searching for Spike. I waved at him, and he left the other ghosts on the other side of the parking lot and made his way toward me. "Hey. Can I ask you to check something for me?"

"Sure, what do you need?"

"Pepper just brought up the fact that the barrier keeping you in Mystic's End should be down. Since you know where it is—or was, can you go check? See if you can cross it?"

Spike nodded. "Sure, Plum and I can go check it out. The edge is just a mile north of here."

Without waiting, he turned and grabbed what I assumed was his new girlfriend. The two made for the tree line.

"Hey, I have another question," Pepper said slowly, gazing after them.

I raised my eyebrow.

"Why was he not sucked into the crystal ball prison with the rest of the town?"

Her question gave me a start. There were only two ghosts—well, three— that didn't wind up in a witch bottle or the crystal ball prison. At least as far as I could tell. Miss Bessie, the mailman Tom, and Spike.

Miss Bessie was the mystic before me, the heir to the power the coven had spun up to counter whoever cast the curse. Though she and I had never talked about it in-depth, we assumed the residual mystic power she possessed kept her from going wherever the rest of the town had gone.

Someone had smashed Tom on the head with a crystal and accidentally trapped him within it. I suspected his murder actually saved him from the curse, held him there when he should have been deposited in another crystal somewhere else.

But they killed Spike. Just plain old killed.

"I don't know," I told her. "Maybe once we know more about what's going on in that church, I'll be able to figure it out."

* * *

"It's down, baby!" Spike hollered as he and Plum raced toward me. "There's a lake on the other side of the boundary? And I could never get to the other side of the boundary to get to the lake? And I just went across, and I could get to the lake!" Spike panted breathlessly—which always amazed me. How do paranormals without lungs gasp?

The other ghosts stared at him, their eyes wide with excitement. "You're sure?" Miss Bessie called.

"Didn't you just hear what I said about the lake?" Spike's head cocked to one side.

Dalida and I exchanged a long, speculative look. "That means there's another step to free the ghosts in prison. It's not as simple as removing the magical boundary surrounding Mystic's End or breaking that part of the curse."

"What about Anna?" Pepper asked. "Could she be powering their prison? Or, like, the reason the door is locked?"

"We have two magical imprisonments left. The human ghosts in the crystal ball and a witch encased in selenite. It's basically a chicken or egg situation, now, I would think," Dalida suggested. "Is Anna keeping the ghosts locked in the crystal ball, or are the ghosts keeping Anna imprisoned? Or are they both tied together somehow?"

"Maybe she's free already," I said absently.

I noticed that Martin, a few feet away from Gabe and Chris, held still. He was listening intently.

"Nothing in this endeavor happens

spontaneously, Fortuna," Pepper told me. "That would be too easy for something as protected as that hole."

"Yeah, I guess you're right," I admitted.

Martin's head dropped.

I covered my eyes with one hand, trying to collect my thoughts.

Though I knew the crystal ball was probably in the church—and I was sure it would be challenging to convince the churchgoers of what they'd been doing—I hadn't figured out the next steps I needed to take.

To be honest, I was secretly hoping the uncorking of the last witch bottle would magically set everything right, at least from the curse's perspective.

And if that didn't work, I hoped that Karen becoming a dog coupled with uncorking the witch bottle might also do the trick.

No such luck.

Pepper's voice was puzzled. "Remind me again, how did you free Tom from the rock he was locked in?"

"Weren't you with her?" Dalida asked.

"I was actually kidnapped at the time," Pepper told Dalida with a wave of her hand. "You should've seen Fortuna and the guys. They came in

guns blazing and fingers fidgeting to rescue me."
Pepper smiled. "It was awesome."

"He just needed to know why he died, why he
was killed," I told Dalida. "It was almost like a
haunting, you know? Once the ghost understood why
his death happened, he popped right out. I don't think
that's going to work here. Tom imprisoned in the
crystal rock was an accident. These people?" I waved
toward the church. "These people were deliberately
shoved in that rock. There has to be a barrier around it
that we're going to have to take down."

A barrier we have to take down...

I turned and looked at Angie.

Then my eyes narrowed.

"What?" Pepper asked. "I know that look.
What's that look?"

"It can't be that simple," I murmured.

"What? What can't be that simple?"

"Fortuna, what are you thinking?" Dalida
asked, looking back and forth between Angie
and me.

What I was thinking was Spike never made it
into the town crystal ball. But more than that—
when I bought the building, Spike hadn't left it for
almost twenty years. He'd tried to escape and
bounced off the walls like he had his own personal
Mystic's End cursed boundary. The ghost had even

gone to the roof and attempted to jump off. No dice.

I thought it was his own psychological barrier, something he had put up.

But because my sister, Angie, had accidentally pushed him down the stairs?

I wondered.

"Angie!" I called, breaking away from the group and heading toward my sister and her father. "When you pushed Spike down the stairs, do you remember anything specific happening to you? Feeling anything, seeing anything?"

"Fortuna, we just found my mother in a witch bottle." There were tear stains on Angie's face, and her complexion was pale. "You just told me my dog is a murderer. Now you want to bring up a painful moment from my past?" She stared at me. "Are you mad at me, and I don't know it?"

"Far from it, Angie. I am sorry I have to bring this up. But it could be important."

"It was years ago, and Spike forgave me!"

"I promise you, I'm not doing this to cause you any more pain, but I need to know. You know a bit of what magic feels like now. I need you to think really hard and remember that moment." I stared into her eyes. "Remember that panic you felt when you saw Spike? When you pushed into him?"

Angie's face churned with emotion. "Did you feel any magic, any energy? Think hard."

My sister mopped at her face with one hand, smearing the tears from her cheeks. Pepper and Dalida joined us. "I was freaked out, Fortuna. I was scared that he would call the police and my father would find out; I was terrified that I would go to jail. I was scared I would never get out of town, never get away from my mother." Tara Clutterbuck winced behind her. "And when I pushed him, I only meant to get him out of my way." Her eyes watered again, tears escaping. "When I saw him falling backward, everything went white. There was this kind of rushing in my ears—"

"That's it! Angie was the one that cast the protection over that building," I told Dalida, cutting Angie off. "That white that you saw, the roaring in your ears? That was magic. You didn't know what you were doing, and when you tried instinctively to protect Spike as he fell? You threw out way too much energy. So much you basically sealed the building."

"I don't know, Fortuna. It seems like one heck of a reach," Dalida responded, her tone doubtful.

"It's not. Look at her natural powers. She can take away pain. Now, how would you do that if you don't actually heal the thing that's hurting?" I asked my twin, eyebrow raised again. "What does a painkiller do? It numbs nerves, right? It doesn't really make the thing that hurts stop hurting by fixing it. It just blocks it so you can't feel it."

"You think she puts a barrier around whatever the painful thing is?"

"I do. For her, the painful thing that night was happening in that building. And so she blocked it. Instinctively."

"I don't understand," Pepper said, her face confused. "What does that have to do with the people in the crystal ball?"

"It's a boundary," Dalida explained. "It's a similar type of magic. If Angie can put them up, she can also take them down."

I nodded. "We each seem to have particular strengths in one area of magic. I think Angie's—"

"Wait a minute! Wait a minute, wait a minute," Angie said, turning pale. "You don't think I'm the one that has to release all those people from the crystal ball? I didn't even know I was a witch three months ago! I don't know how to do any of this! I just touch people, and something happens. I can't control it!"

"But Fortuna can," Dalida said, nodding toward me. "She's a telepath."

"Well, that would be fine and dandy if she had..." Angie trailed off, looking back and forth between us. "Hold up. You want to come in my head and unlock the crystal ball through me?" Angie asked. Her expression was both fascinated and appalled. "Can you even do that?"

"Look, we just came up with this idea. I haven't thought it through." I wasn't even sure Dalida's idea would work. Even though I was the only one out of the three of us that had been turned into a full witch, I'd never worked with any boundary magic before. Not the boundary magic that could imprison a multi-generational town of ghosts in a ball.

"Well, start thinking," Angie's mother said as she walked up. "You've got me out of the bottle. Angie and Terrance have had some time to adjust to the shock." The small woman looked at me sternly. "We've been milling about here for twenty minutes. It's time to bring this to an end. For everyone."

* * *

"And that's all I know," Ollie finished. He hadn't gotten as much information as I'd hoped.

When Ollie and Pepper had showed up at the church, Reverend Kane was surprised—and suspicious. Ollie had left the church and moved out of his father's house on the very day his father declared it was time for him to join the men's group.

Since Ollie refused—and left—he'd never been told precisely the purpose of the men's group.

It was clear now the church existed as if it were a typical congregation—albeit one with an irrational fear of paranormal and mythological creatures. Many people attended the church not understanding that it was funded by Karen White or that the men's group passed a magical crystal ball around. Many men, nearly all women, and all children were kept in the dark.

"They know we're coming?" I asked him.

Ollie nodded. "I tried to talk to my father, come clean with some of what I knew. He accused me of being bewitched, controlled by paranormal forces." The assistant coroner shrugged. "He was pretty nice about it, though. No one grabbed me and tried to burn me at the stake, so I don't think anyone's going to get violent. But no, he didn't want to believe me that Karen was evil. He's convinced what the men's group has been doing was right." He tilted his head. "I didn't know about the crystal ball thing to tell him about that, so he doesn't know."

"It's too bad they can't talk to the people in the crystal ball," Pepper said to the group. "Maybe those folks could convince them it's not a great place to spend eternity."

Light bulb.

"Well, why can't they?" I said, a sly smile

spreading across my face. I looked at Dalida, and she half-smiled. "Dalida can do it. Maybe. If she can't, she can at least make the ghosts we have with us visible."

"Are we sure the ball is even in that building?" Gabe asked.

"Beau's mother is in there talking to Prunella and Bond Noble," Pepper told Gabe. "There's a bowling ball bag next to him on the floor, and he won't let it out of his sight. I tried to get close to it, but he's really twitchy." Pepper shrugged. "This church doesn't have a bowling alley, so I think it's in there."

Chief Clutterbuck and I looked at one another. "We still don't know who killed Conrad Noble," he said.

"Or why," I added.

"Or what any of this has to do with that piece of property the church wanted," Pepper added.

"Actually, we don't know that the church wanted it," Clutterbuck added. "We just know it was deeded to the church for some reason."

"I don't know that you're right about there being no possibility for violence, Ollie." Gabe glanced toward the church building. "I know you grew up in this place, and it doesn't seem threatening to you, but someone was shot in the face for that crystal ball. Not to mention the distillery that was deeded to the church—whether the church wanted it or not, it clearly has something to do with all this. These people killed someone over this stuff."

"Well, we don't know that, either," I disagreed with Gabe. "We didn't get very far with the investigation into Conrad Noble's death. We don't know if any of those things have to do with why he was killed."

"All I'm saying is we may be here for a specific purpose, but let's not lose sight of the fact that there might be a murderer in that building." Gabe stepped closer to Dalida. "And that murderer? He—or she—might have a gun."

TWENTY

Everyone was tense.

Adults gathered in small groups around the darkened room, just a handful here and there. Some laughed nervously, others stared with tough-guy expressions, and one older woman in the corner cried quietly at the sight of us. A man next to her patted her hand. The crying woman nodded and pursed her lips together.

"They're terrified," I whispered. Maybe I was telling the others what I sensed. Perhaps I just wanted to give voice to their fear. Either way, my body flooded with tension I was sure was only partly my own.

"Be careful," Chris murmured, his unblinking

eyes scanning the room for threats. "Frightened people sometimes do unexpected things."

The multipurpose room (which I hadn't been in previously) was almost as large as the chapel on the other side of the building. Large windows lined it, but heavy drapes covered them to keep out the moonlight and prying eyes.

"Reverend," Clutterbuck called out across the room.

Reverend Kane glanced over his shoulder, sighed, and stood up from one of the tables. He turned, slowly, to face us. "Chief, what brings you out here to the church so late at night?" His eyes swept over our group, and for a moment, the preacher's face tensed upon spotting Ollie and Pepper. "And with so many faces I wouldn't expect to see in your company."

"They don't belong here," Beulah Conroe shrieked as she thrust herself up from a chair in the northwest corner of the large room. "None of you people belong here! You just go home now! Shoo!"

We didn't move.

She continued to glare accusingly until she spotted her son, Beau. "Beau!" All conversations halted. Angry red splotches colored Beulah's cheeks. "Beau Conroe, what are you doing with those devils? Come over here now, young man!"

The detective blushed in the face of his

chastising mother as the soft, distant rumble of thunder soundtracked the bizarre confrontation. "Mama, I think you need to listen to these folks," he answered smoothly—though he didn't step toward her as she demanded.

"I don't listen to devils!" Beulah spat back. She slapped the table in front of her with her hand. "Come over here, boy, and get away from them! Don't make me tell you again!"

"Now, Beulah, some of these people are friends. That's no way to treat kin, is it?" Reverend Kane told her. "Clearly, they're all here for a reason, so perhaps we should listen to what they have to say." Turning toward me, he raised an eyebrow. "I take it this witching-hour visit is your doing?"

He looked...hopeful.

Why would he look hopeful?

I tried to isolate Kane's inner world from the fear and panic swirling around him.

Reverend Kane wasn't sure of himself...and he was doubly unsure how he should react to us. On the one hand, he sensed the situation was not a good one for him—though the Reverend couldn't quite put the finger on why. But he knew my mother, and he knew of Beulah's passed-through demand. Had I visited Karen White, he wondered. Would the church funding flow back toward him?

Perhaps I had been sent here on her behalf, he thought.

"Actually," I responded, ignoring the fearful eyes from all corners of the room, "I think you'll find by the end of the night this may be partially your doing, Reverend Kane. The crystal ball your men's group is protecting? It's more than it seems and far more than you've been told." I paused and waited, expecting an argument or an outburst, but none came. Despite their fear, they were listening. "It's not some religious object. It's a prison."

"It is not," Beulah scoffed, but she hugged herself with her bare arms. "Don't you listen to these people! They're liars and devils! What have they ever done for this town besides cause trouble?"

"Besides," Bond Noble said as he stood up and pointed at me, frightened by what I just said. My eyes widened when I read the same knowledge within him I was trying to tell the group. But how would he know? "It's not a crystal ball! It's an orby-culum! It's a holy object that only the most pious and favored of men can safeguard, and—"

Pepper rolled her eyes. "That's another name for a crystal ball, you dolt. *Orbuculum* is Latin. Orb, and..." Pepper looked around. "Actually, I don't know a lot of Latin. What is *culum*? Doesn't it meant butt?"

"I hardly think so!" Beulah shouted hotly. "How dare you!"

Chris met her gaze. "*Culum* is seen in English as -cula, or -cule. It's a diminutive suffix roughly translated as 'to make small' or 'somewhat smaller.' *Culum* is also the masculine version. *Cula* would be the feminine." The vampire paused and tilted his head. "Though it can also mean buttocks."

"You people need to get out of here!" Beulah snarled.

Outside, the far-off storm grew closer, and it howled.

Inside, more silence. More glances across the room.

Footsteps whispered on the polished floor as the separate smaller groups gathered together into larger ones. I wasn't sure whether it was for comfort or defense, but I figured it was probably both.

"Should we just expose the ghosts?" Dalida asked quietly. "Maybe that will help them understand."

"Fortuna, that may be the quickest way to move this along," Miss Bessie agreed.

Dalida reached into her bag and tossed out dozens of small crystals with a swift movement. The rocks tumbled across the floor and skittered across the large room.

"What are you doing?" Beulah shouted.

Dalida whispered amid a deafening clap of thunder—and with that, the descendants of the witches of Mystic shimmered into view of the townspeople that worked so hard to ensure their continued purgatory.

* * *

"Bessie," Beulah choked, staring with horror at the only ghost she knew well. "Bessie Baker, you don't look a day over fifty. How did you get so young?"

"I died." Bessie swept her arms back toward the other ghosts. "It's not an age-defying trick any of us would recommend, but there are a few benefits to moving into the next phase of existence." Miss Bessie straightened her shoulders and looked back briefly toward the Reverend. "Now that you see we're here, maybe someone should bring out that crystal ball so we can get on with this. We're not the only ones."

The gathered parishioners looked left, looked right, looked up and then down. Some were pale and shaking. A few seemed to mouth prayers. Others stood, shocked, their mouths open wide as if frozen in a scream. I observed (with some admiration) a calm Reverend Kane.

He was not pale, and he was not shocked.

But he also wasn't speaking.

"The crystal ball needs to stay where it is! It's the only thing that protects us from the likes of you!" Beulah said, flaring her nostrils in a fury. "We were warned that someday you would all come back, that you would come to destroy us!"

"My mother told you that," I said quietly to the old woman. "Karen White gave birth to me, and then abandoned me. She did the same to Dalida." I gestured toward my twin and then glanced at Angie, not wanting to divulge her secret.

I understood Pepper's point about secrets being toxic, but I wasn't ready to jump in the "never hold my tongue" boat with her. Angie clung to her father, Martin behind her. As our eyes met, she gave a quick nod as permission.

"Our younger sister Angie's story is, in some ways, even worse than ours."

Gasps from the crowd. Half looked at Angie while the other half scrambled for a better vantage from which to view her.

"Angie was adopted?" Hoyt Abernathy stepped out from behind a tall man. Angie's face softened.

"This town has a lot of secrets," Clutterbuck told Hoyt. "More than just Angie's. It's time for all that to stop now."

"And in all the ways that are important, Hoyt

Abernathy, I am Angie's mother," the shimmering Tara told Hoyt.

"Does any of this really matter?" Bond Noble asked with a patronizing toss of his head. I looked at him. Something within him had shifted rapidly. Too rapidly. "We were told what to do with these people if they showed up—just the way they have tonight. I don't know why we are bothering to have a conversation with any of them. We all know what to do, don't we?"

"Bond, wait—" Reverend Kane said, but it was too late.

The assembled church members reached into purses, grabbed jars from behind them, and pulled handfuls of something from their pockets. With a not-at-all unified shout of "Be gone!" they all flung something wet and foul-smelling in our direction. It all happened so fast that only Chris reacted quickly enough.

Like the vampire hero he was, he flew across the room, gathering those of us alive into his arms as he tried (best he could) to block whatever it was.

Which turned out to be garlic.

Well, not just garlic.

Apparently, when you tell many older women (and men), they should get as much garlic as possible to protect themselves? The best deal to be had on garlic was the gigantic jars of the minced stuff at Costco.

Because that's what poor Chris was covered in.

Once the aerial attacks ceased, Chris released us from his grasp and stood up. The indescribably exasperated look on his face told me he had absorbed most of the attack. I wrinkled my nose as he came closer to see if I was all right. The stench of garlic was enough to make my eyes water, and I tried not to gag. "My apologies for the odor," he said. He pulled his garlic soaked shirt off and attempted to shake the globs onto the floor.

"Oh my," Mary, Gabe's mother, said breathlessly, looking Chris up and down. Leaning toward Miss Bessie, she whispered loudly, "I'm beginning to understand what Fortuna sees in the vampire. His chest looks like it was chiseled out of marble."

"They can all hear you, you know," Miss Bessie told Mary.

Mary shrugged.

"That's a vampire?" Reverend Kane choked out with a cringe. He grabbed wildly behind him as if looking for something. Whether it was a weapon or something to lean on because he was having trouble standing, I didn't know. He was frozen to the spot and seemingly unable to move. Unable to think.

A witch walking into his church didn't faze

him. Ghosts appearing, the dead talking? No big deal. A vampire ten feet from him? That, apparently, got his attention.

"But we just covered you in garlic! Why aren't you dead?" The big man suddenly looked gaunt; his eyes opened so wide they were the most prominent feature on his face. "Garlic kills—"

"Garlic doesn't kill vampires. In fact, the traditional belief is that garlic's odor deters vampires. However, even that's not true in a metaphysical sense," Chris told the Reverend, still shirtless. "We have hypersensitive noses, and so we have an aversion to anything that smells particularly pungent." Chris rolled up his shirt and handed it to me, gesturing toward his back. I wiped off the last of the garlic as he continued. "Most of the rumored vampire repellents have a perfectly obvious—and non-lethal—origin."

A man pulling thick silver-rope necklaces and bracelets from a pouch he was carrying stopped and stared at Chris. "Silver?" he asked nervously, holding up the jewelry.

Chris shook his head. "Like I said, most of the rumored 'instant death' mechanisms don't work."

"Oh yeah?" Bond Noble asked. Then, the unmistakable sound of a revolver being cocked. "How about a bullet, vampire? Is that a rumored instant death mechanism?"

* * *

The parishioners were suddenly more frightened of Bond Noble than they were of Chris.

Which, since he was a vampire and Bond Noble was a member of their church?

Well, that seemed odd.

"Bond, you need to put that gun away right now!" Prunella Noble, Conrad Noble's widow, grabbed his arm and pulled, but he shook her off with a sneer. "Bond, that's the chief of police over there, you idiot! And the detective! You're going to get yourself arrested!"

"The chief of police is over there with witches and vampires," the scruffy man told his sister-in-law contemptuously. With a mocking laugh, he shoved her away. "I told you that I was better at this than my brother. I should've been a member of the men's group years ago!" Bond glared at Reverend Kane. "But no, you wouldn't let me in until I got you that stupid land. Well, I'm in now, aren't I, preacher?" He uttered a crazy laugh.

"Bond, this is a church—" Reverend Kane started, but Bond cut him off.

"This isn't a church. This is your personal piggy bank, and I finally figured out how to make it mine." Bond paced back and forth across the rec room, waving his gun wildly as he spoke. "You've been using Karen all these years, taking from the church coffers. I figured it out. I figured it out!" He paused and shrugged. "Well, I met someone from Las Vegas, and they told me all about it. Big biker dude that used to work for her. Anyway, I know what you were doing. Oh, I know more than any of you idiots!" Bond's gun waved toward the terrified Holy Grove Church parishioners. "Maybe even you, Reverend!"

Chris met my eyes and tilted his head toward the gun, but I shook my head no. Pepper caught the exchange and murmured in surprise, but I surreptitiously pointed toward Bond then tapped my ear. Glancing at Clutterbuck, he nodded his agreement and then looked to Chris. "You're fast enough, right?" he whispered.

Chris looked shocked at the chief's implication and his trust. But he shifted into a slight crouch all the same. "I guess we're going to find out," the vampire whispered back. Turning to me, he muttered, "You get behind me."

I did.

Just as my sister stepped in front of me.

"Tell me what you knew," Dalida said, her voice low and her demeanor cool. She stepped toward Bond with steady steps, her arms wide. "You're so smart; surely you want to tell me what you did."

She tilted her head coquettishly and sighed contentedly. "I mean, you're smarter than any of them, right? Tell them. Tell them so they can appreciate your...your genius."

"Yeah, I am a genius, right?" Bond replied proudly, his eyes glued to Dalida.

Pepper, startled, moved toward Dalida. "What the—"

I grabbed Pepper's arm.

"Her powers are the exact opposite of Fortuna's," Miss Bessie told Pepper. Before she got two words into the sentence, Dalida flicked her wrist, and the shimmer surrounding the ghost dimmed.

"Where did she go?" Clutterbuck asked, frowning.

"Can you still see me, Pepper?" Pepper nodded. "Much better at her magic. Good girl, Dalida. Anyway, remember, Fortuna can go into someone's mind and see what's there, yes?" Miss Bessie told Pepper. The reporter nodded again. "Dalida can do the opposite. You can see me because Dalida has enabled your mind to perceive me on this plane. She's not doing anything to me so you can see me." Miss Bessie extended her hand. "She's doing it to you."

Pepper looked surprised. "But I don't—"

"Hush, child, Bond Noble can still hear you. I

don't know how strong her hold is over him." The older woman glanced over her shoulder once again to check that Dalida was still the center of Bond's rapt attention. "Dalida realized that Bond Noble had a plot of his own, and she's appealing to the parts of him that want to confess. That wants people to know. She's helping him, magically, to believe that everyone here will be in support of him. Now, let's listen."

"—so when Reverend Kane, here, told me that Conrad wouldn't sell him the old distillery, I knew I had an in." Bond was sitting casually on a table, swinging his feet. The revolver sat next to him on the table, still within inches of his hand. He looked pleased that Dalida was paying such close attention to his story and he was cheerfully animated. Like he was relating a trip to a favorite ice cream shop. "Joe Bob told me Karen was twisting this whole town up, and he told me all about the people she had imprisoned in the orby-culum. An orby she convinced these idiots was some kind of blessed protection thing!" He slapped his hand hard on his leg and laughed uproariously. "Can you believe that?"

"What are you talking about?" Reverend Kane asked fearfully.

"I ain't talking to you, you idiot!" Bond shouted

fiercely, his face twisting with rage. "I'm talking to her!"

The Reverend shrank back.

"Yes, Bond, you're talking to me," Dalida told him. She reached out and took him by the hand. The anger drained from his face, and he turned toward her with a smile. "Please, finish the story."

"So, Joe Bob told me about Karen and that she was using this stupid town to power her magic. He mentioned someone here had taken her down. That's how Joe Bob was able to get free. I knew she had been arrested, and I knew my brother and his stupid wife were all wrapped up in this church. Conrad was even one of the people that guarded the orby." Bond frowned slightly. "I told him what Joe Bob told me, about Karen being super-wealthy and giving this church all this money—money that the Reverend just stole. I told him we could step in, we could help her, and then she would probably give us all the money after kicking Kane out."

I stared in shock. I didn't like where the story was going.

Yet another disaster with my mother's hand in it.

"So I went to see her in the jail, and she told me that she needed the land next to the church and my brother wouldn't sell. That if I could get my brother to sell, she would get Reverend Kane to make me the top man in the men's group. That once I had the ball? I could knock that idiot off his perch and take over, and then all the bonuses would be mine!"

"Your brother wouldn't sell the family land, though, would he?" I asked from across the room.

"So you shot him in the head," Clutterbuck followed.

"Well, I didn't really want to," Bond told Clutterbuck, though his expression told a different story. "But Prunella wanted to be the top woman at the church. She said it wasn't right that Beulah Conroe ran over everybody like a big fat—"

"I beg your pardon!" Beulah Conroe shouted angrily.

"Yeah, she said you didn't like her much. Prunella and I had been having an affair on and off for years so it wasn't all that hard to get her to agree." Bond laughed. "She thought my brother was boring. And Prunella did own half of the family land, so I kinda needed her help. But yeah," he agreed, legs still swinging happily. "I was the one that shot my brother, and just to show Karen how dedicated I was, we donated the land to the church! For nothing! I knew she had to make me top man then!" Bonds looked around proudly. "When Karen finds out everything I did for her?" Bond picked up the gun and thrust it toward the churchgoers for emphasis. "You all are going to be bowing to me!"

"You look terribly tired. That must've been exhausting, pulling off all of that." Dalida reached forward and gently placed her palm on Bond's cheek. "You should sleep now. Your eyes, your lids... so very heavy. Here, let me take that," she said as she gently removed the gun from his hand.

As soon as she had a firm grip on the handle, Dalida held it out behind her. Gabe ran forward and took it.

"Yes, Bond, sleep now."

Bond Noble, the murderer, slumped over on the table and snored.

TWENTY-ONE

"Clutterbuck is taking Prunella de Vil to jail, too," Pepper said as she rejoined us in the multipurpose room. "He said the prosecutor and judge can sort out who's who and what's what."

Chief Clutterbuck removed Bond Noble from the church without incident, while the shocked churchgoers stared silently. Though it felt like the evening was over, no one else left the premises other than the chief, the unconscious murderer, and an enraged Prunella de—um, Noble. The parishioners stood, staring—as if waiting for something more to happen.

"Dad doesn't want you to wait for him to come back," Angie told me.

"That's good because it's already almost one o'clock in the morning." Gabe looked around the room. "It takes a while to process people into lockup, so he probably won't be back for hours. Whatever you're going to do, I think it's time you do it."

With Clutterbuck gone, I wasn't super enthusiastic about jumping into the next phase. Out of all of us, he was the closest to Reverend Dexter Kane; I was counting on having him here to lend some calm to the situation. Well, Ollie was close to Kane, too, but one glance at my friend's face told me he wasn't super enthusiastic about breaking the truth to the assembled crowd, either.

"Do you know why we're here?" I asked Ollie's father.

He swallowed nervously. "We've been told that, at some point in the future, the paranormals that were kicked out of this town years ago would come back to take their revenge." Kane ground his teeth as his eyes moved over us. His gaze stopped on Chris. "We were specifically warned the attack would be led by a vampire. So, that would be my first guess."

"A vampire you said we could defeat with garlic, and look at us now!" Beulah spat at Kane, her fist descending on the table with a loud bang. "We covered that thing with garlic from head to toe, and

he's still standing there! Shirtless! Defiant! Alive!"
The woman next to Beulah, the one previously
weeping, let out a low moan as if she was in pain.
The old woman shot her an annoyed glance. "Oh,
stop that, Gertrude! If that vampire doesn't like the
smell of garlic, he's certainly not gonna drink you
first! You eat so much of it, I can smell you ten feet
away!"

Gertrude flung herself back in her chair and
glared.

Chris stood up straight and pulled his
shoulders back. "No one here has any ill intent
toward any of you. Especially not me. We did not
come here to harm any of you. Whatever you may
have been told, whatever you've been led to believe
about us? We are not here to exact any kind of
revenge."

As I listened to my boyfriend, I felt my breath
catch in my throat. Gabe's mother was right; Chris's
chest did look like it was chiseled out of marble.
Goodness, my boyfriend was smoking hot. And he
was such a nice guy.

You know, for a bloodsucking vampire.

Damn vampire dazzle.

"This church was founded on the idea that the
world needs defense from you people. That this
town needs a defense."

"Magic just saved all of you from a gun-toting

madman," Chris pointed out. "Dalida risked herself to protect you."

"And you could do to us what you did to him!" a woman shouted from the corner. "Would we even know it? Would we even know you were in our minds, controlling us? Making us do evil things? Reverend Kane, you're the one that told us about this." She turned to him, a pleading look in her eyes. "Reverend, what do we do?"

Reverend Kane cast a wary eye toward Chris, then turned toward the woman. "Beverly, I...I've seen and heard things tonight..." He looked down and then turned toward Ollie. "Is what you said earlier true? Was Karen just using us?"

Before Ollie could answer, Mrs. Conroe started up again.

"Well, it sounds like you were using us, too, Reverend," Beulah spat. She marched out from behind the table toward the church leader. "What was Bond Noble going on and on about, about you taking money from the church? Did you really make that man part of the men's group because he gave you land?" She took a deep breath, but before Kane could answer, the old woman lobbed another question at him. "And what was so important about this land, anyway?"

Reverend Kane took a deep breath, his eyes closed and his face turned upward. With a forceful exhale, he nodded to himself, lowered his head, and faced Beulah Conroe. He was trying to maintain an air of bravado, the stance of a man still in charge, but the attempt was a failure.

"Karen said there was a large selenite deposit beneath the old distillery, and she wanted it. The distillery was built on top of an old quarry, and there's an untapped and unknown deposit of crystal. At least, that's what she claimed," Reverend Kane told Beulah. "She needed to get that land so that she could use it..." He trailed off.

The words Ollie tried to get him to believe ran through his mind like a train, so loud I could hear them without effort. He looked down again. "She directed me to give Bond the position if he got us the land. But I swear to you, Beulah, it never occurred to me he would murder his brother for it. Or that Karen was trying to replace me with that psychotic f—"

"There are ladies present, Reverend!" Beulah snapped before Reverend Kane could finish his thought.

"Oh, Beulah, the man murdered his own brother after sleeping with his sister-in-law," Beverly told Beulah brusquely. "Whatever that F-word was going to be, it was probably mighty appropriate."

"This is still a church," the old woman countered. "I still don't understand—"

"As much as I think you all have a lot to talk about—and I am sure you do have a lot to talk about—we didn't come here for a church social," Pepper interrupted abruptly. She strode across the multipurpose room like a woman who knew exactly where she was going. Reaching a table, the reporter leaned down and snatched up the bowling ball bag left unattended amid Conrad Noble's arrest. "Now, whether you all believe it or not? The crystal in this bag isn't some magical protection amulet for Mystic's End."

"Of course it is; we've been guarding it for years," a man in his mid-fifties told Pepper.

"You see that ghost? And that one? And those two over there?" The ghosts waved as they were pointed to. "They've been locked in little tiny bottles. Some for twenty years, some for a hundred years, and some for even more than that." Pepper unzipped the bowling ball bag and pulled out a stunning white crystal ball.

The church members gasped.

Palming it, Pepper held it up in front of her. "You see this ball? This amulet that you've been doing some directed ritual around?"

Beulah gaped at Pepper with a mix of mystification and fear, perplexed that the reporter had not been struck down by lightning or felled dead by an instant heart attack.

A quick focus on the mental murmuring clarified where the expectation came from. Apparently, they believed women could not touch the crystal ball. With a thundering bolt of clarity, the pieces fell into place.

The descendants of witches were all women.

This misogynistic church separated women and men to keep women away from the *orbuculum* prison.

"This crystal ball houses every ghost of every townsperson that's passed away," Pepper called out. "They are all locked in there together, and you people have been getting together to do some kind of magic ritual to tighten the front door lock."

"That's impossible! We weren't doing magic!" Beulah told her, looking horrified.

"You were participating in a magical imprisonment," Pepper argued back, her eyebrows arched fiercely. "Karen mentioned you guys were keeping the ghosts alive or powered up or... something. I don't know. But I don't know any religion that has a ritual around an object that is imbued with some kind of symbolic properties—"

"Catholic mass and communion," Beulah told her, her hands on her hips.

"The Latter-Day Saints and that Celestial

Room," Beverly added. Beulah turned and raised her eyebrow at the other woman. "What? I saw it on HBO. It was stunning. All white. It was just lovely."

"That Jewish swimming pool thing—" a man said, but Pepper cut him off.

"Okay, okay! Just trust me. You were participating in magic!" Pepper said with exasperation. "For goodness sake, I don't know how you people wound up at this church with as much as you seem to know about religion. None of you questioned for a second whether these beliefs were ridiculous? Seriously?"

"Okay, there's no need to be insulting," Reverend Kane told his likely future daughter-in-law.

"I'm not insulting. You people really have basically been certifiably crazy."

"Wait a minute. Didn't you come in here with a vampire? And don't you write that pagan-heathen-occult blog?" Beverly asked Pepper.

"That meticulously researched, unbelievably well-written pagan-heathen-occult blog?" Pepper responded proudly. "You bet. That's me. And boy, are you people going to make a great entry. And my blog never imprisoned hundreds of people's souls."

"Fortuna, I'm not trying to be rude, but we are

running out of moonlight," Chris said loud enough for most to overhear.

"So that sun thing can kill you, then, huh?" a formerly silent man asked quietly. Chris favored him with a look so cold the man seemed to stop breathing as he shrank under the vampire's withering gaze. Then he coughed. Then stepped back. "Ah, I was just curious. Since we're all chatting, you know. Nothing intended by that observation." Chris continued staring. "Um, sir."

At that, Chris smiled warmly, his fangs faintly visible. "Of course. No intention inferred."

The man shuddered.

"Are we going to do this, or what?" Pepper asked, holding the crystal ball out toward me.

"Do what?" Reverend Kane asked.

"Free the town." I stepped forward and gently took the crystal ball from Pepper. "We freed the living." I turned and looked at Angie. "Now it's time to free the dead."

* * *

For something that had been so profoundly woven into such a complicated conspiracy, freeing hundreds of ghosts was far more straightforward than I would've believed. Angie, Dalida, and I spent half an hour walking around the crystal ball, discussing different attack plans with Miss Bessie and Mary. Once we determined our magical action course, we placed the ball on a small table and stood at three points around it.

We grabbed hands, and—

There was no explosion, no flash of light, no screaming.

All the plans we had, all the spells and chants we would try?

None were needed.

Just a fraction of a second passed between our hands clasping and the first tiny speck of light floating up and out of the ball. Then there was another, then another, then another. Eventually, it looked like a spray from a Fourth of July sparkler. We stared as the dead of Mystic's End left their prison.

"I'm not even concentrating on anything in particular," Angie whispered. She looked at me with a worried expression. "Am I supposed to be thinking something? Doing something?"

"I don't think so." I looked across at Dalida. "I'm not really concentrating on anything, either. Are you?"

"I don't think this is a spell. I think the three of us, being here, was the key."

"That must be why you kept running into magic working to keep you away from these things,"

Angie said as her eyes followed a pink spark. "Why would Karen have such an obvious hole in her spell?"

"I don't think she put it there," Miss Bessie said, her hands clutched in front of her chest as if in prayer, her expression jubilant. "You girls are, for good or ill, her daughters. Her blood runs through your very veins. But she shoved you away, all three of you." Miss Bessie, standing outside the circle, unclasped her hands to put her arm around Mary. "Karen never understood the bond between mother and child. So how could she account for it? I doubt it ever occurred to that narcissistic woman the three of you would be anything other than what she thought you should be."

Dalida, Angie, and I looked at one another. I felt both of my sisters squeeze my hands. I squeezed back.

The multipurpose room grew crowded, the air cool as ghosts and specters expanded and took form. Those we rescued from the witch bottles were hard at work greeting those newly freed, explaining where the town had been and what had happened to them. The churchgoers, still able to see the dead in their midst, stared in shock.

"Mama!" a woman screamed, and then a sob. "Mama, is it really you?"

It was Gertrude. She was the first to recognize a

family member, but she wasn't the last. Soon the air was filled with laughter, tears, excitement. Shouted greetings, hollers of joy. Reverend Kane stood off to the side, a conflicted look on his face. Relief flowed from him that the damage had been reversed, but he was mortified he had played a role in what led to this.

"Dexter?" a small, shy woman in a yellow sundress whispered. "Dexter, it's me."

The woman swept toward him, excitement on her face.

Reverend Dexter Kane stared as if he couldn't believe what he was seeing. His eyes filled with tears.

Finally, the ball stopped its spray of glittering soul stars.

"I think that's it," I told my sisters. We swept the ball with all of our combined psychic senses, and one ghost even volunteered to go back in and ensure everyone made it out. "We got everybody."

"Not everybody," Martin Salvi said, staring at me with a pointed look. "Anything else here can be taken care of another time. You have one more person to rescue."

"Fortuna, do you need us to come?" Dalida asked me.

I nodded. "I don't think it can hurt."

I knew there would be many discussions about

Holy Grove Church, its parishioners, and their role in the curse. At least some townspeople now knew that real witches and vampires walked among them. I didn't know how much influence this night would have on their future attitude toward me, toward Chris. Toward paranormals in general.

But that could all wait until tomorrow.

I owed Martin one last rescue.

* * *

"I can see the hole," Dalida said, shivering in the darkness. "There's really someone down there?"

"Encased in selenite, yes." I frowned. "What the heck was it with Karen and selenite?" Karen-dog barked happily and wagged her tail. Gideon barked in response. "Maybe Gideon will be able to teach her how to send images, and we'll know eventually. Selenite is such a pretty, happy stone. Hard to believe it's been used for such misery."

"Anything can be used for good or evil, you know," Angie told me as she leaned down and stared into the darkness. Straightening, she shrugged. "So, are we all going down? You want us to wait?"

"I can see the hole, as well," Martin said, his voice vibrating with nervous energy. "When Chris took me out here the last time, he pointed to where it was, but I couldn't see a thing. That's good, right?"

"The curse is broken now," Chris said. Then he frowned, looking worried. "Anna was being kept alive by the magic that powered the curse. If that's the case..." He trailed off, glancing at Martin for one second. Saying nothing else, the vampire dove down into the hole and disappeared.

Chris shouldn't be worried, I thought. She's fine. She was safe in...

A sudden fear washed over me.

"Let's go!" I shouted and scurried down the ladder into the darkness.

The candles and fire that showed the way previously were no longer illuminated. My heart thumped in my chest, a faint whisper in the back of my mind droning repeatedly that we would be too late, that the woman at the heart of the rescue that freed an entire town would be my mother's last victim.

"Stop it," I muttered to myself as I descended deeper into the darkness.

"Stop what?" Dalida asked. "I can't see anything."

I held up my palm and whispered several words. A tiny ball in my hand flared into incandescence.

"You need to teach me how to do that," Angie called from above.

Suddenly, hands gripped my waist and pulled me off the ladder.

"I reached the bottom, but I don't see a door. Where's the door?" Chris asked me frantically.

An agonized shout from Martin.

I placed my hands on the cave wall where the entryway used to be. It was just there, open, for me the last time I was here, so I wasn't sure what to do.

The last time I was here, Anna led me to her chamber, too. She talked as soon as I climbed down the ladder, mind to mind. I think.

She talked me through getting to where she lay, imprisoned.

Now, her voice was silent.

"Oh, God, please, just open," I whispered, the fear overtaking me as I banged against the stone. "Please, please. Don't let me fail at this."

As if by magic, the cave wall disappeared, and I spilled into the pitch-black chamber. With rapid-fire movements, I flung balls of light in every direction to illuminate the room.

"She was toward the back wall!" I shouted and ran in that direction. "This way!"

A strange hush fell over us, the sound of our feet shuffling against the floor the only sound. I made my way to the ledge and...

...I stopped short and stared.

The selenite had shattered.

It lay around Martin's mother like shards of glass from a shattered window. Anna was pale. If she was breathing, I couldn't detect it. "No," I whispered. "No. Oh, God, please, please. Please don't let us be too late. Please."

A frantic Martin was struggling behind me, shouting questions.

Dalida and Angie held him back.

"Let her work, Martin!" Angie shouted, but Martin was beyond hearing anything.

I reached out tentatively, Chris by my side, and touched her cheek.

At the slight pressure from my fingers, an agonized wail escaped Anna's lips. "Fortuna!" she gasped.

"Mother!" Martin shouted.

"I'm here! What can I do? What can I do to help?" I pleaded with her. "Tell me!"

She moaned, and her face contorted into an expression of agony. Gasping, Anna shook her head. "You could never save me. I knew it, always knew it. I've been locked in here for years." The woman, scarcely alive, choked and coughed with the effort to speak. "I knew when I told you what to do, but the others had to be saved. You all had to be saved. She had to be stopped."

"Stop it!" I demanded. "We're not going to let you die! I have to be able to do something! Anna, tell me, I'll do anything!"

Anna moaned again in pain, her suffering etched into every line on her face.

"You stay here, Martin, do you hear me? Just stay here with Dalida!" Angie tore herself away from Martin, her healing power useless against the depth of his grief. "Let us try and help her!" Without waiting for his agreement, she ran over to Anna and placed her hand on the woman's shoulder.

The gaunt, almost ghost-like face relaxed and Anna exhaled with a wheeze. "Child, that's a wonderful power you have," she told Angie. "My son is lucky to have you. Take care of him. He was never willing to accept my death." She breathed in deep as if savoring the air. "Help him to see that it's all right."

"No, Mother!" Martin Salvi, a rich, tough guy, sobbed as he pulled away from Dalida and came face to face with his mother for the first time in decades. "There has to be a way to save you! I didn't come this far only to lose at the end! I did this for you! I did this all for you!" His eyes swept over her skeletal body, the damage from her imprisonment clear. Anna's muscles had wasted away, her skin pale, her hair brittle. "These are powerful witches,

Mother!" Martin looked up at me, his mother's hand clasped in his. "I've seen you do amazing things. You have to be able to fix this!"

"I don't know how," I whispered, the despair overwhelming.

"Martin, I'm the healer, and all I can do is make it so she doesn't feel pain," Angie told the love of her life stoically as tears ran down her cheeks. "I don't know how to fix what's been done to her. I'm so sorry."

"NO!" Martin roared. "This can't be how it ends!"

"Martin," Dalida whispered, her arms wrapped around him. "Martin, you may only have a few moments with your mother. Don't spend them fighting against the inevitable."

Martin stared at Dalida, his face lined with horror. He lowered his head gently against Anna and whispered how much he loved her, that he always knew he would see her again.

"So, perhaps not entirely inevitable," Chris, standing at the end of the stone slab, said quietly. Martin's head snapped up as he looked at his friend. "I can bring her over. The vampire blood can heal pretty much anything." He looked down at Anna. "I know you don't know me, and I don't know how much you know about being a vampire, but—"

"Do it," Anna told him, her face confident. "My

life was stolen from me thanks to Martin's father—much as yours was—and I know more than you think. You've been a good friend to my son, a better friend to him than his father was a father." Anna paused as great, wracking coughs overtook her. After a few moments, her raspy voice wheezed, "I'd be honored if you would make me a vampire." An amused smile danced on her thin, dry lips. "And frankly, imagining the look on Marty's face when he sees my fangs? It's the first thing I've got to look forward to in a very long time."

Chris looked at Martin and raised an eyebrow.

Martin stood up and stepped back. Hope danced in his eyes.

Then he nodded.

And that's how I wound up watching another woman suck on the neck of my boyfriend for several hours.

TWENTY-TWO

It wasn't quite finished, but it felt finished.

Making a vampire is a time-consuming thing. We stayed huddled in the cave into the morning and on through the rest of the day. Anna fell into a breathless sleep after drinking her fill of Chris's blood, and for a bit, I was nervous. Eventually, within hours, her hair grew fuller, and the color slowly pinked up her pale cheeks.

"When will she wake up?" an exhausted Martin asked at least once an hour.

"I told you. The sun is up," Chris would remind him sleepily as he dozed in the corner. "We sleep during the day. Just let her rest, Martin. When the moon rises once again, she'll open her eyes." He would sigh and close his eyes, hoping to dissuade Martin from asking the question again.

Which he always would.

Sometime in the afternoon, Miss Bessie floated in with another ghost I didn't know. I yawned, stood up, smiled, and greeted them despite the weariness clinging to me like a shroud.

It was the tenth person that day.

The ghosts from the crystal ball had scattered almost immediately to all corners of the town in search of relatives, descendants...and, okay, a few seemed excited by the concept of "haunting" someone that wronged them in life. A few returned to the church to thank me. Miss Bessie staffed the multipurpose room and floated them into the cave. We chatted quietly in the corner for a few moments, and then they would fly off.

"Martin, get some rest," Angie told her boyfriend as he sat up restlessly and looked over toward Anna. "You're going to be up all night talking to your mom, I'm sure. Take the chance now to recover." She pushed him back against the wall and settled his jacket around him like a blanket. "You don't want me to start experimenting with my powers to see if they can knock a person out, do you? I will. Don't think I won't."

"You must be exhausted, too."

"I'll rest tonight when your mother wakes up.

It'll give the two of you some time alone. Now, sleep."

Martin settled fitfully on the rocks. Gideon walked over and crawled up next to him. Soon his breathing was rhythmic.

"Our men are as stubborn as the day is long," Angie said as she picked her way back over to Dalida and me.

"Mine's snoring," Dalida responded with a chuckle, glancing back at drooling Gabe Wilcox, his head resting on the back of the greyhound Bella. Ollie and Pepper were curled up beside him. "I think he fell asleep before anyone."

My mother was lying on her back, paws up, in the center between us.

"She looks so peaceful," I said as I watched her barrel chest rise and fall. "What are we going to do with her?" I looked up. "Can we take our mom to an animal shelter? I mean, we can't just drop her off as abandoned, can we?"

Angie tilted her head. "It would be a karmically fitting end to our relationship, wouldn't it? She abandoned us, so we abandoned her?" Angie frowned. "It just doesn't seem right, though. I don't want to be the type of person that would do that. She would do that. I'm not like her."

"I'll keep her," Dalida announced as she reached out and petted the dog's soft fur. "You guys both have dogs, and I'm the only sister that doesn't, so...I don't know, it kind of seems like it was meant to be, doesn't it?"

I shuddered. "I don't think I ever want to hear that phrase again."

Despite my psychic powers, I never could have predicted today. I didn't foresee my mother, or my two sisters, or an entire town of the dead locked in a ball—a vampire boyfriend.

Despite Miss Bessie's insistence I was the mystic and destined to set it all right, I couldn't have done it without the people in this cave. Humans and witches, the living and the dead...everyone worked together.

Even Clutterbuck.

And I really couldn't have predicted that.

Maybe it wasn't meant to be, but I was grateful it came to pass all the same.

* * *

"Why didn't anyone offer to make me a vampire before?" Anna asked, enamored with her speed and strength. She whizzed from one side of the cave to the other, stopping periodically to lift large boulders and then place them down gently. "The feeling of freedom is absolutely incredible!" She looked over at Chris. "Thank you so much!"

He gave a quick nod.

"Mother, we really should get everyone out of this cave. We've been here all day, and the sandwiches Dalida brought back were not all that filling," Martin said as he put his tailored jacket back on. "I'd also like to call my father and let him know—"

"Oh, no," Anna said fiercely, pointing her finger at her son. "I realize I've been out of the picture for over twenty years, but Marty is still my husband. I'll deal with contacting him if and when I decide it's time. For the moment, I just want to enjoy being able to move again." She shook her tangled halo of strawberry blonde hair and gazed hungrily toward the door. "I may not be able to see the sun again, but the night air... the moon..." Her eyes lit up with excitement. "Come, my son. Accompany me on my first step of freedom."

Pepper looked back and forth between Chris and Anna. "Is it my imagination, or is she suddenly talking kind of like him?"

"We vampires do seem to have a mode of speech that tends to be a tad more elegant than you humans," Chris told her. "It's not something we pick up over time, just something inherent in our nature."

"Uh-huh. You have an exquisite way of insulting people, too." Pepper raised her eyebrow. "I'm inelegant, am I?"

"I meant no disrespect," Chris responded kindly, He silently put his hand over his heart and gave a slight bow.

"Man, you just can't rattle that guy, can you?" Pepper chirped, following Martin and Anna toward the exit. "Martin's right though, I really am starving. Speaking of starving," Pepper glanced toward Anna, "does she know not to eat people? Well, at least not people we like?"

Chris nodded. "We'll head back to Martin's house. There'll be food for all of us there."

Anna and Chris ferried the dogs up the ladder and out into the night. We followed much more slowly.

I was a little disappointed I didn't get to see Anna's first impression of the night sky. By the time we reached the surface, the new vampire was running around the clearing. She was so excited by the moon, then the stars, then the wind.

She couldn't erase her smile, and it was contagious.

* * *

"Where were all of you today?" Clutterbuck asked. He arrived accompanied by a sheepish-looking Reverend Kane. "I was getting worried. I came back to the church, and all of you were gone. No one could find you."

They joined us on Martin's patio overlooking the glittering town. The moon, full and bright in the sky, bathed it in a silvery-white glow. Uncle Vito brought out plates of Italian dishes while Aunt Addie and Anna sat off in a corner. They spoke animatedly in hushed whispers, and once in a while, peals of laughter echoed.

Chris and Anna sipped something from metallic tumblers.

I didn't ask what it was.

No one else did, either.

"Chris turned Martin's mother into a vampire," Pepper blurted out between bites of lasagna. "She slept for a few hours after drinking all the blood and stuff, and by then, it was the middle of the day. You know the whole thing about vampires and day and sun...actually, maybe you don't." She pointed at Reverend Kane. "Since you told your parishioners to pick up minced garlic from Costco and toss it in case of an emergency." Her eyes narrowed. "Did I mention we were in a cave with the vampire all day? The vampire that was covered from head to toe in wet garlic? In a small cave? With no ventilation? Because of you and your dumb advice?" She let out what sounded like a growl. "Thanks for that."

"You slept the whole day," I pointed out.

"And I dreamed about garlic the whole time," she countered. Pepper shook her head and then took a bite out of a slice of garlic bread. "Had a nightmare I was swimming in the stuff."

"My apologies again for that," Chris told her.

"Wasn't your fault. Was his fault." Pepper jerked her chin toward the elder Kane.

I snuggled up closer to him and breathed in deeply. I didn't know what magic he used in the shower, but if it came in a bottle from Bed Bath and Beyond? I wanted some. Chris smelled fantastic, not even a whiff of garlic anywhere on him.

"How are your parishioners doing?" I asked Reverend Kane.

"They are actually more upset with me regarding my salary than they are with what they saw last night," Kane said as he shifted uncomfortably in his chair. He glanced across the table at his son and then dropped his eyes. His expression was slightly embarrassed. "They weren't aware that my salary was as high as it was, and the board was quite upset when they realized had I been paid less? Well, we wouldn't have needed Karen quite so much."

"They're not freaked about all the ghosts they saw?" Angie asked, surprised.

"We believe in the paranormal, so much so that we worked to contain it," the Reverend responded. "Most of them are really excited that they got to finally see something supernatural. They're rubbing it in the noses of the people that didn't come to church last night." He chuckled. "Beulah Conroe says last night was a revelation. Of course, her mama was one of the people stuck in that ball, and I think they had a few words before Dalida left and the ghosts disappeared." Reverend Kane turned toward Dalida. "Speaking of which, some of our members have asked if you'd be willing to come back so they could finish the conversations they were having."

"It didn't even occur to me the ghosts would all disappear as soon as I left," Dalida told him. "I mean, I should have, but I didn't realize. Of course, and please let them know I'm sorry."

"So what happens now?" Angie asked.

Clutterbuck shrugged. "None of us live under Karen's thumb anymore. The ghosts go wherever they want? We all stay away from Fortuna when we're thinking about something no one else should know?" Clutterbuck leaned forward and scooped some baked ziti onto a clean plate and then leaned back in his chair. "I expect Reverend Kane's church will have to make some adjustments."

"That's an understatement," he murmured.

"I don't think there's much more to uncover," Clutterbuck nodded. "Maybe we all just get to relax and get to know one another. I think all the secrets have finally been dug up." He looked at Angie. "Your mom, by the way, would like to talk to you later. Before she disappeared, she said a few things to me that I think you should hear."

Angie tensed and swallowed. "Like what, Daddy?"

"Like that she loves you. There's more, but that was the gist. I still think you need to hear it from her." The lawman winked at his daughter.

Her eyes teared up, and she nodded.

Chris abruptly pulled away from me and pushed out his chair. "Excuse me for a moment." He turned and disappeared through the french doors before I could ask him where he was going.

"What happened?" Martin asked, confused.

I stared blankly toward the closed doors and bit my lip. "I don't know, but I think I'm going to go find out."

* * *

After wandering through the mansion, I finally found Chris in front of the house, looking at the parked cars.

I coughed discreetly, even though I was sure he heard me calling for him in the house. He turned and smiled faintly, then turned away again. I frowned. "Hey, are you okay?"

He nodded without turning around. "I'm fine."

"You don't seem fine." I walked up behind him and placed my hand lightly on his shoulder. He turned swiftly and folded me into his arms, his hand cradling the back of my head. "Oof, goodness, that was unexpected." He squeezed harder. After a few moments of weighty silence, I got even more worried. "Okay, as nice as this is, now you really don't seem fine," I said, my voice muffled because my mouth was smashed into his right pectoral muscle.

He chuckled and pulled back just enough that our eyes could meet. "I love you."

"I love you, too." I waited, but he said nothing in response. "Chris, you're starting to scare me a little. What is it? We accomplished everything that we were trying to do. Everyone's okay. I mean, we're having a party on the veranda in celebration of how awesome we did." I tilted my head back further. "Why do you not look like what we did was awesome? You look like you're very much not feeling awesome." I blinked, and a nervousness gripped me. "Is it Anna? Is there something about you making her a vampire I don't get?"

"No, no," Chris answered, smiling. Then the smile faded. "It's not what happened in the last twenty-four hours. Well, it is." He took a deep breath. "Seeing all of those people greeting their families, how happy they were to see one another... it made me wonder if I really needed to cut myself off from my mother and sister."

"Oh, Chris," I sighed, drawing him closer. "You did what you thought was best. Don't beat yourself up."

"I don't think you understand." He reached for me, his hand cradling my cheek. "I never married, I never took a woman home and told my mother I was in love." Chris smoothed an errant hair from my face and outlined my lips with his finger. "I never wanted to until I met you, and now..."

"You feel you can't because they think you're dead."

He nodded. "I'm really struggling with what to do next, here, Fortuna. I isolated myself from them for their own safety because Karen was dangerous. And yes, I did what I felt was best. Yet now I find myself wondering if there are still reasons to do so."

Tears sprang to my eyes as I listened to the pain in his words, and in response, he looked away. "I want them to know me. To know you. Now that they are no longer in harm's way from Karen, I...I don't want to cause them pain. I don't know how they'll react to what...what I've become."

"You're still you. No matter how much you've changed, you are still you. And they love you. And they're probably fantastic people. They couldn't be otherwise," I told him, smiling. "Because you're fantastic people."

"This coming from the woman whose birth mother was a sociopathic murderer and whose adoptive mother was a rapacious egoist." I blinked, shocked at how on the nose he was. Chris was right. I didn't know if his family would accept him, and I didn't know if his desire would just cause him more pain. They could be awful people.

But I had hope.

I nodded sheepishly. And then I frowned. "Oh my God."

"What?"

"You've got to be kidding me!"

"What is it?"

I pushed him away and pointed. "I just realized I don't even know your last name!"

"Of course you do," he frowned. "I'm sure I've told you."

"I'm pretty sure you have not," I disagreed. "For months, I knew you as Jeeves. Then you asked me to call you Chris. But that's as far as we got. That was it. What the heck is your last name?"

"Have I honestly not told you?" he asked himself quietly. "Amazing. Perhaps you're right."

"Well?" I asked, tapping my foot.

"Trevino."

"Your name is Chris Trevino?" I asked. He nodded. "What's it mean?"

"You know, funny you should ask that. Aunt Addie looked it up once. It means 'lives at a place where boundaries meet.' Kind of cool, huh?" I nodded. "Do you like the name?" I nodded again. He smiled slyly. "So, how much do you like the name?"

Then he leaned down and kissed me.

* * *

"Everything good?" Martin asked as we returned to the patio.

Chris nodded. "It's fine, Martin."

"It is not, we just realized—" Pepper started, but Ollie's hand shot out and covered her mouth forcefully.

I glanced around the table.

The expressions were somewhat...shell

shocked. "What did we miss?"

"Have some wine, Fortuna," Martin said, jumping up to pour me a glass. I glanced around the table again and noticed Dalida and Angie were pale. "Red? White? A Scotch, perhaps? I have a wonderful—"

"Somebody better spit it out," I warned Martin. "What happened?"

"Fortuna, you really should take some wine," Angie said, exhaling.

Pepper finally ripped Ollie's hand away and spoke incredibly quickly, so quickly I had trouble following. "So, Clutterbuck asked who the head witch was in the whole mob witch paranormal army thing, and Martin told him that Karen was actually known as the head witch. And then Clutterbuck mentioned that during the whole...thing, Clarissa, the witch, was supposedly the daughter of the head witch. Or, at least, that's what Martin's father said. So, he asked Martin if Clarissa was actually Karen's daughter, which, if she was, would make Clarissa your sister. Well, not just your sister," Pepper finished as she pointed at Dalida and Angie. "And I said that would make sense because, in witchcraft, there are four elements—"

"I...wait...what?" I looked at Chris. "Was Clarissa...is Clarissa Karen's daughter?"

Chris exhaled. "Maybe. I don't know if Clarissa

was adopted or...I don't know."

"Who would know?" I asked him.

Everyone on the patio stared at Karen, the dog.

"Well, that's not a lot of help, is it?" Dalida said with exasperation.

"She can't be our sister," I insisted.

"Why not?" Angie asked.

"Because she was a complete moron!" I crossed my arms and glared at the dog. "Is there any point in my life where you are not going to be making things more complicated for me?" I shouted.

"There is someone else who would know," Martin said, his face drawn tight. "My father." Martin looked over his shoulder at his mother and Aunt Addie. "At some point, I'm going to have to go back to Las Vegas. I don't want to let my mother face my father alone." He swallowed. "To be perfectly honest, she would probably eat him. Anyway, I could ask him and find out for sure. Clarissa is there. Or she was, at least, before everyone scattered."

I looked at Chris. "Your family is in Las Vegas, aren't they?" He nodded. "We could go for a while. I'm sure Martin and Angie would let us stay with them until you decided what to do."

"Of course, Fortuna, you and Chris are always welcome," Angie assured me.

"Martin and Angie?" Clutterbuck said. He

turned to look at his daughter. "You're going with him to Las Vegas?"

"Dad, I'm rich. You know how it is to be a rich person in Mystic's End? Well, being a rich person in Vegas?" she tilted her head. "Way better. You could come with us. You love poker. You've always talked about competing in the World Series of Poker. I think they have it there."

He stared at her in horror. "I can't afford that!"

"Oh, Daddy, I can afford it ten times over." Angie leaned into Martin. "But, yes, Dad. I go wherever he goes."

Martin smiled and kissed her on the forehead.

"You're all leaving?" Pepper asked, crestfallen. Ollie grabbed her hand and squeezed.

"Look, we don't have to decide any of this right now," I said as I sat down in my chair with a thump. "We just got a break. Let's take that break. Finish everything that we've got going here, and then figure out what we're going to do next. Let's give everyone time to recover."

"Well, what I'm gonna do next is drink some of this Scotch," Reverend Kane said as he stood up and headed towards the liquor cart. "All these problems? They'll still be there tomorrow."

I sighed as Chris sat down next to me.

Somehow, they always are.

But at least I didn't have to deal with any of them alone anymore.

* * *

THANK YOU FOR READING!

I hope you enjoyed Captive Magic, the **final** book in the Mystic's End Mysteries! You can go back in time to The Magical Midway series, or move on to the next series in this universe, The Owl Star Witch Mysteries!

Fortuna, Gideon, and Chris will be back! Join the newsletter for announcements!

KEEP UP WITH LEANNE LEEDS

Thanks so much for reading! I hope you liked it! Want to keep up with me?

Visit leanneleeds.com to:

Find all my books...

Sign up for my newsletter...

Like me on Facebook...

Follow me on Twitter...

Follow me on Instagram...

Thanks again for reading!

Leanne Leeds

FIND A TYPO? LET US KNOW!

Typos happen. It's sad, but true.

Though we go over the manuscript multiple times, have editors, have beta readers, and advance readers it's inevitable that determined typos and mistakes sometimes find their way into a published book.

Did you find one? If you did, think about reporting it on leanneleeds.com so we can get it corrected.

www.ingramcontent.com/pod-product-compliance
Lightning Source LLC
Chambersburg PA
CBHW021443240626
47153CB00001B/275